THINKWELL BOOK

HOMA
& O

Jeff Weston wa _..in in 1970, in Bolton, Lancashire. He graduated in 1999 from Manchester Metropolitan University with a degree in English literature and commenced a career in stockbroking the following year. He is the middle son of an electrical engineer and barmaid/housewife and author of three novels (*The Leaf Blower*, *Mutler*, *Wagenknecht*), three plays (*The Relationship*, *Directions*, *The Broken Heart Ward*) and a collection of short stories (*Homage to Hernandez & Other Stories*). His writing has crossed over into sports journalism and book reviews / feature articles for psychotherapy magazines.

On Wagenknecht:

'Editors and agents have become more boringly cautious than ever…I admire your ambition'

-Peter Buckman, *The Ampersand Agency* / formerly of *Penguin Books*

'The underlying premise here is imaginative'

-Sophie Lambert, *Conville and Walsh*

'You write well'

-Tibor Jones & Associates

'From start to finish, very difficult to put down, desperate as the reader is to salvage and assemble the bits of meaning percolated through the narrative. *Wagenknecht* is a courageous, bold and inventive piece of modern literary fiction'

-Ade Kolade

'The earthy and intellectual gab of William Wagenknecht shows irreverence, revelry and bite'

-Patricia Khan

'As if Roth, Bellow and Salinger have risen from the grave and, together, planned one final project designed to purge modern culture of its vacuousness'

-Sean Thomas

On Homage to Hernandez & Other Stories:

'Heraclitus said that a man's character is his fate. True enough, but only when our traits are laid bare by others do we understand just what it means'

-Andrew Routledge
(Modest Anger)

'A cutting and poignant take on a difficult period of my life'

-Anon
(The Pictures on the Cabinets)

'Blimey – it's very good, but incredibly sad'

-Gary Spencer
(The Pictures on the Cabinets)

'Loved it. You are a genius!'

-Manjulla Dhir
(Jelly & Ice Cream, Jolene)

'This is a collection of stories for the hermit, the dissident, the disenchanted, the apostate, the freethinker, the iconoclast, the heretic – all those people that life tries to throw in a ditch'

-Jeff Weston

Jeff Weston

HOMAGE TO HERNANDEZ & OTHER STORIES

THINKWELL BOOKS

Written by Jeff Weston 2009-17.

Support and proofreading by L Hernandez.

Cover design & interior formatting by Rachel Bostwick.

Published by Thinkwell Books, U.K.

First printing edition 2019.

For my baby girl

MAY I WANDER

in your memory always

"To shut out feeling lonely,
I get out of my head

Lost everything around me,
Not dealing with it well"

- John Newman,
Out Of My Head, Tribute

Naivety (2012)

He didn't realise there were crooked fences. Nor blades of grass that failed to point up to the sky. He didn't realise there were sad couples sat in station waiting rooms – their lives not expected to be great nor fulfilling nor able to turn the tide. He didn't realise that Muslims hummed in what seemed like a melancholic and poignant address to the Gods. He didn't realise that human evolution often meant a dip in kindness.

He had been protected – taught little which might upset him or give him cause to worry. There had been no politics in the house – just a formal history by way of his father's New World Library collection. When they sat down to tea the overriding concern was whether his mother had bought a packet of six cakes or five; the latter meaning he would have to share the extra slice with his older brother. If girls phoned the house after seeing him on his paper round, they would be dealt with firmly by the interjections of his mother; their keenness deflected and deflated. He was to be green in the ways of the opposite sex – left to stare in wonder at their peculiar habits.

But then came the day of his 'release'. He hadn't been altogether stripped of human interaction before this. An adjoining back field with the neighbours' children had meant games in the summer and snowball fights in the winter. The shout was never far away though – almost psychically before deep connections were made. And so he skipped back – entered the bastion land of his parents' creation. College was to absorb him now, however – place its frazzled hand on his shoulder.

'There may be incidents with which you're unfamiliar, George. Smoking. Drinking. Larking around. Some of this from the brighter students as well. Don't feel obliged in any way. There will always be someone of your ilk to discuss things with.' His father had been robust, yet tender. It was quite an ambiguous statement in many ways – far from insistent. He wasn't saying don't join in but rather trying to sterilise the scene for his son.

'I think I know who to trust and who not to.'

'Oh. How?'

'From people in the field. And family members.'

'I wasn't aware you'd got close to any of the neighbourhood children.'

'I haven't. But their actions. Sometimes bravado precedes them. Also, they form units of power...seem to give up their higher thoughts in doing so.'

'Remarkable.'

'What is?'

'The way you speak, despite…'

'I'm not with you, Father.'

'Just sit down. Sit down, please. I have to tell you this before you set out.'

'This is making me a little nervous.'

'Don't be. You ought to know a few things, that's all…now you're sixteen. Two years away from university.'

'OK. What like?'

'Me and your mother…we've carefully cultivated how we've raised you. Tried not to expose you to this modern world with all its traps and vices.'

'I know that already, Father.'

'I'm not sure you know to what degree, what extent though. I feel quite deceitful telling you now as if this is *The Truman Show* or something. You remember me enthusing about that film? Talking about the sadness I felt, not when he escaped, but throughout the film? I think because he quietly knew there was something more out there.'

'We feel that in the real world as well.'

'Yes. Quite an irony. Have you felt it, George?'

'I…I look at maps. Think of travelling. Wonder what kind of people live beyond the British Isles.'

'I've travelled in my head mostly. Apart from the old Yugoslavia and Spain. Your mother never did like planes. Preferred the roads. And now, we don't go far, as you know.'

'What was it like?'

'What?'

'Yugoslavia.'

'It was...very rural. But then we mainly peered out from the hotel grounds and saw the roads on the way from the airport.'

'Did the experience change you?'

'It was a big thing in the eighties flying abroad. It meant more than it does now. As for changing me. Well – swimming outside every day. Feeling the heat. Chatting with people who seemed ever so kind.'

'Foreigners?'

'Yes – those who worked in the hotel. Less grumpiness all in all.'

'Why do you think that was?'

'Part of it was obligation, I expect – working in the hospitality trade. But another more special part struck me – there wasn't the cynicism in their eyes.'

He looked at his father whose world had somehow stopped turning and felt prone to a similar descent. Before...before his own world had even begun. Sadness enveloped a man – tipped his mouth downwards. But what – what was there beyond this house?

His paper round had brought him the most interaction. He saw, through the differently designed paths leading up to the houses, that England could never be a fascist country. He saw, in the faces of people he handed papers to on summer days, that all they wanted was peace and a garden. Speaking to some of them – rude not to when traipsing on their land – he gleaned fragments of happiness. It *was* leaning into Thursday evening when he saw these people on his weekly run though. How could anyone be sad on a Thursday? Just one more day of work. Pity the Monday Evening News boy who had a different slant on the world.

'I'll drive you there if you like.'

'That would be...' So not to hurt his father, even though something had risen up in him vehemently stressing that independence was now the order of the day, he spoke the only word possible: '...nice.'

'If you've got your stuff, we'll go then.'

There couldn't be fear or a sense of foreboding on the way, in the pit of George's stomach, because people were pleasant. Really pleasant.

Argumentative or spiteful people had never been to the house. Perhaps for that reason they – according to the laws of probability – didn't exist. The bravado that he had witnessed in the back field was likely limited or purged once they approached full adulthood. The odd heretic was understandable. It depended on and correlated to a person's expectations matching their day to day life.

George thought as the car moved that he had never been allowed to answer the door. Even as a fourteen- and fifteen-year-old. And for that matter had never been in the house alone. The one crisis which had prevailed upon them – his mother having a small stroke two years ago (her speech all of a sudden slurred and heartbreaking) – was handled by his father, immediately insisting that the family get into the car and make their way to the hospital. Upon arriving, they were met by quite an unsympathetic receptionist. 'Sit down and we'll assess her shortly.' 'She's had a stroke. Half her face is paralysed. I'd like someone to see her *now*.' 'We all have to wait our turn, sir. With respect, you're not a doctor.' 'I'm not a...*what*?! You doubt me? You doubt anyone's ability to read what's happened here??!! I've known my wife for twenty-five years, seen every expression of hers, but never this, and you say I'm not a doctor!!'

Nothing was 'now' anymore after that. His father had shifted tracks – permanently. He had been mortally wounded by this unfeeling woman before him. 'Why give people like that jobs in this environment? Christ – who does the hiring? Let's just headhunt Beelzebub and have done with it!'

They pulled up outside the college. It had started to rain. His father placed his chin on top of the steering wheel. 'I used to do this, you know – hide behind the rain drops. Occasionally put the wiper on and recover the world. Stare at the first person to come into view.'

'Getting away,' George responded.

'Mmmm. They criticised us, you know. Friends. For being protective. For wrapping you and Charlie up. Said that we were avoiding the inevitable. "Let them fall, John." That's what I got. "It's the only way." I think we've done alright though. Look at you – I'm a proud man. No glue sniffing or drinking or anger. A young man curious about the world. It's alright saying that Einstein was a rebel, Frost a prankster – and look what became of them – but they're the exception. Bums' names don't surface. They don't.'

'Dad – sorry, but I'm gonna be late.'

'Of course, son.' He pulled George to him – kissed him on the forehead. Left a hand on his shoulder, almost asking that his son grapple, exit from the fatherly womb by dint of his own strength. George dipped his head, opened and closed the door and then proceeded through the gates of the college.

It was a large institution. Not a pretty or classical or gothic face to it, but rectangular building after rectangular building. He had only been here once before. On 'Open Night'. The staff seemed congenial – keen to talk about the wider campus rather than just their individual subjects. George had managed to purloin a good chunk of time from two of his main tutors: Mr Beckford of the Spanish department and Mr Gooding – History maestro.

'Was Spanish a favoured subject or stocking filler for you?'

'It's something I've chosen with my father in mind.'

'He's Spanish himself?'

'No. No. I'd like to act as his escort through South America one day.'

'Because of his love of the continent?'

'He mentions it occasionally. But it's more to do with returning his smile.'

'You think travel will awaken him?'

'I think anyone who sees Venezuela, Bolivia, Argentina, Chile can't help but find their fight again.'

'Does he know of your plan?'

'No. I'll tell him two years from now.'

'That's certainly one of the finest reasons I've come across for signing up to my course. Let's hope you do well, George.'

'Thank you. I aim to.'

It still played in his mind. Almost embarrassingly so. Cards on the table. It somehow wasn't the western thing. How to pull away from that though? At the same time – why lessen his candidness? He saw little bits of others each day which seemed to barricade him in, restrain that bursting from him. His rather stiff lessens in history had added to the malaise, hence his need to seek out fuller descriptions of the past.

'You intend to give me the orthodox play on events or something more, sir?'

'Just what are you asking?'

'The victors' words – I feel they might have suffocated me from an early age. What have you done to mitigate this?'

'The source material *is* often narrow – that I grant you. Stating that Columbus, for example – through his violence – was merely a product of his time is unacceptable. What I will give you – some of it out of necessity, off the record – is...walk this way, George...'

They moved away from the tabled area with its bright, welcoming signs, up a flight of steps and into a deserted class room which looked out over the vast playing fields.

'I like areas of land not built on, George. I was lucky to get this room. I can breathe in here. We're all stifled by something. Your questions are admirable but I know of some teachers here who would see them as a little impudent, disrespectful even.'

'Oh. I didn't mean to cause offence.'

'I see that in you. You're at an age where people expect a degree of deference though. This is no longer a simple power relationship, a pedagogical march, but something more delicate and enigmatic.'

'Tell me something, Mr Gooding.'

'Yes?'

'When I eventually write the answers to the exam questions, how much leniency will the examiner give?'

'By "leniency" you mean will he or she pay heed to the set answer or reward points for a grasp of the subject no matter what the conclusion?'

'I do.'

'Something too out of the ordinary and you might have a problem. Intelligence usually shines though. Do what you need to do. And if we need a re-mark, I'll be in your corner.'

'Good,' George nodded. It was interesting where you could take a conversation even without a great bank of knowledge.

Now, in his mind, he pictured Beckford and Gooding, along with Mr Dawson, his law tutor as he approached the college's outermost door. Their faces loomed large. They would respond to his sensibilities or try to smash them – perhaps fail to honour their original words. George noticed the gleeful expressions of those around him, the keen gait of the crowd. They didn't seem like big drinkers, or addicts or glib individuals as his father had quietly warned, but instead a rather optimistic and earnest set.

There was to be a half-hour induction in the main hall. A welcoming pitch. A run down of the college's achievements, its *Who's Who*, followed by a speck of rules and regulations. It all seemed quite fair and magnanimous. George applauded at the end, unlike the group to his left whose hands barely touched or grazed each other.

They examined him. 'Inspired?' one of them asked softly.

He wasn't sure how to respond. This was more sophisticated than what he was used to in the field. He turned his head towards the speaker and the people around him. And then recoiled, turned back without any words. There's a few of them, he thought – but it's not a dumb exchange. He repeated the young man's question in his head: Inspired? Was he? Was he really, particularly after making demands on Gooding? What he was listening to – wasn't it just piffle? Didn't the fellow have a point with his obvious sarcasm and the boundless layers within that word?

'It's only polite,' George responded, neither meeting his, their demands with a true answer, nor fulfilling the requirement to adopt an adversarial tone.

'I think you should join us tomorrow. There's a time-honoured initiation ceremony in the car park at the back. I know because I've had brothers here. Game?'

Another one-word question. George picked at its four letters, its synonymity with hunting. Perhaps that's what they were doing – hunting an obvious loner struggling to take flight or gallop fast enough. He decided to nod. And in quite a supercilious fashion ill-befitting him.

'Five o'clock.'

Nothing more. Nothing further. As if they hadn't spoken at all. George noted the somewhat late hour. There would be hardly anyone around. An absence of witnesses. He tried to focus on the stage once more – the rapping up, the new faces coming into view. But...What on earth had he agreed to? How would he explain away not being on the 407 bus to his parents?

The insouciance slipped a little. It was hard to maintain the composure which his nod had suggested. Of course I'll do your bullshit initiation, his body had said – jump a couple of bushes or something – but now, he was tightening up, wondering what horrors would befall him.

The day came. His lessons had taken him away from the portent that jutted his mind. He learned that there had been the Speedwell boat and not just the Mayflower in 1620. He learned that of the two Italian 'anarchists', Ferdinando Sacco was probably guilty of murder, Bartolomeo Vanzetti not. This contained him for much of the day, along with an interesting Che Guevara speech Beckford had prepared – asking that the pupils translate it and understand its power at the same time. Law was a little less interesting with Dawson – quite formulaic and unexceptional - but overall he had had a gripping day. One to savour. Offer juices and a swishing roar to the harbour of his mind.

It was later that he began to see them dotted around his classes; parts of the crowd that had been with the cool challenger, the initiation warlord. He made eye contact with a couple, but some of them he could not stand and had to turn away from. Something in their faces was as he'd pictured the bedevilled haranguers at his parents' door – most of them, he had to confess, he'd only seen the slouched, quite hopeless backs of through the window.

This clearly wasn't for him. Deadbeats would only strangle the lustre of what his parents had created. They would accuse him of snobbery as so many did, when really it was their utter lack of direction and purposelessness which drove any conversation into the ground. He had committed though and as such there was honour at stake; something his father had stressed as central to being a man.

'You know where to go?' one of them asked him after classes had finished and the remaining numbers began to dwindle.

'Yes – near the line of trees.' He hadn't realised it before but where he had agreed to meet was exceptionally well hidden from the sightlines of those stood at the college's rear windows. If something happened he would perhaps go unnoticed until the following morning when the stream of traffic in and around the college would resume.

'He's here,' he heard someone say, as he slowly trooped towards them. They seemed close, tight knit – ready to celebrate or mock his exploits.

'OK. Let's start,' he said without feeling or effusiveness.

The speaker ambled forward. 'This isn't just you, George. We wouldn't do that to you. It's all of us. With the exception of the driver.'

'The driver?'

'The man in the Mini. Tom. Just got his licence.'

'So he does what exactly?'

This prompted a laugh from the dozen people stood around.

'He drives.'

'And us?' He feared hearing the answer. He wobbled slightly at the blind commitment which now had a grip of him. He heard the giggles intensifying, felt them, but they didn't quite resonate with him.

'We lie on the roof while he takes it up to about 25. Just one of us at a time.'

He wanted to ask about the accident rates (not that they'd have any reliable data). He wanted to bow out – show enormous disregard for their foolish playing around. Something in him was compliant though. Something told him that he had to get to know these people.

'I get to see a few examples? Technique and so on.'

'Yes, George. Technique. Joey – you getting on?'

One of the longer-haired skateboard fanatics in the group emerged and quite nimbly sprung up onto the roof. 'Hold the sides – not all the fingers. Foot at the back so you don't fly forward.'

Tom looked for the signal from the speaker and then cruised off at a steady pace. George watched, as if observing Mr Dawson explain and demonstrate not just the law but the laws of gravity, cadences, centrifugal force and the immutable line between luck and certainty. This…game was dependent on balance, a degree of showmanship and a hardy concentration.

The skateboarder seemed to be doing well. This was clearly his turf, his vocation, a suitable stage on which to cement his place in the group. George tried taking mental notes: the surfboard position at times; the raising of the head. When would it be him? Fourth to go? Fifth?

Tom drove the Mini back after a slow, arcing curve at the end of the road. The skateboarder rolled himself off and then rubbed his hands together as if brushing off sawdust or the grime from inside a garage.

'You next?' came the speaker's words.

Who was he talking to? thought George. He looked up towards him, their guru and leader. No, he countered. You agreed to a few examples. Not me already. I've hardly seen anything.

'Yes. You, George,' the speaker followed up with as a mechanism of shame.

'But…' He couldn't finish the sentence. He couldn't endure what would fly his way if he asked for a reprieve, a delay even. He stepped forward, an image of his parents suddenly in his mind. He remembered the words "Don't feel obliged". What was he now then? His options had shrunk, frayed at the edges. It felt like Armageddon, being surrounded by insidious rats.

Stepping on the bonnet, he slowly lifted and moved his legs around so that he faced forward on the roof as the skateboarder had. Gripping the sides between the roof edge and windows, he tried to secure himself, minimise the potential for sliding around. There was little in his vision now – just the tarmac ahead. The people seemed to have disappeared. Only his parents again, looking at him from the grass verge. What are you doing, George? they asked. Was this in the curriculum? Will we see you again?

He wept. Openly. Unafraid now to release his desperateness. A girl shouted. The thrum of the engine beneath him was cut.

'Get him off! Get him off there!'

He felt hands around him, trying to guide him down. He had his eyes shut – too embarrassed to let them see his watery pupils.

'You knew it was too early. Why did you push him up to second?'

'I didn't know he was a soft bastard.'

'*You're* the soft bastard, trying to be your brother. Can't think of original entertainment.'

'Well – we got tears.'

She moved towards him. Didn't hesitate to thump the speaker in the face. 'And now yours. Give me yours.'

Through the morass of his own stained face, George just about made out the incident. He had never seen a girl hit a boy before. Not in such a vicious manner. She was neither lithe nor beefy nor obviously truculent. Pretty – yes, but tough.

Perhaps he would introduce her to his parents. Perhaps he would seek a bond with her of some sort. George walked through the lingering crowd. Away from the college. He was better now. Better because of her.

Jelly & Ice Cream, Jolene (2012)

It was a way of meeting her. A way of being close without doing damage to his heart. Every word he spoke to this lady was, in a way, insured – through bluff, horseplay, merriment and laughter.

Underneath it all, he was of course burning, thinking of her all too often. In the small hours of the night. In the evening, absent-mindedly watching television. While on the station platform. Everywhere, in fact, she inhabited his mind.

He had devised The Hug Club as a frivolous mechanism. A way of being with her for at least ten minutes of the day. It meant an innocent intimacy. A soft grappling of her wonderful frame.

They worked – if measured door to door – probably thirty seconds apart. A nudge left and then north from his building and he would be there. Before her. Ready to simply wrap her up in his arms.

No one else ever came despite the club's inviting title. That is how he liked it. And she understood its exclusivity, its tilted charms.

'Let's run away. Sell *your* house to fund it,' he whispered.

'*My* house?'

'Yes. It's the sensible option.'

She laughed. At the folly of it. His audacity. His raving sentences. They both knew it to be balderdash and yet its truth, its credibility, rose higher by the day.

Why not? was the echo inside them. Why continue with their separate lives? Why be happy with scraps, bits, disingenuous pieces of a Herculean love?

'I know that it must seem unobtainable. Too far off. A joke even. But understand my circumstances – please. I can't hope to lessen the immorality people perceive in witnessing a married man show interest (gallant interest, I hope) in a single woman, but there is more to it…'

He fell silent for a moment. Studied her face. He risked unwittingly prompting their demise. An end to the blissfulness they had built.

She hesitated. 'How…how do I know that if you formally left her and we…' She refused to or couldn't say it. '…that you wouldn't do the same to me?'

He admired the question – wanted it to be the first from her lips. Knew that his answer would not be perfect, yet it was something he had thought about, considered, over and over.

'What I have isn't dreadful. I'm not going to say it's old or tired or without good verse. It's more to do with how *you* lift me. I try to fill the days when you're not around, but it's all secondary, superfluous. I haven't known this feeling for a long time. What I currently have just isn't enough when I compare it to being in your presence. Will it fade? Have I painted you as I'd like to see you rather than understanding who you really are? No. I don't think so.'

She looked away for a moment. Realised that the nonchalant giddiness of their early 'letters' and brief meetings was, if not quite ending, then desirous of a more fulfilling plane.

'Who's to say you wouldn't want to move on again?'

'There's nothing insidious to my changing direction. It's all serendipity and wanderlust.' I have a four-year batting average, he felt like saying. 'I should ask are you brave enough to hook up with me, to want to commence our trip, but that would assume you have an interest in being together...'

She stared at him. Couldn't quite get a handle on who he was. There were things about him that intrigued her, made her smile, but beyond the playfulness...it was quite nuanced, not something she'd encountered before. Would he demand too much of her? Throw his seamless sentences at her without regard for the earthy necessities of life?

'I can see that you're not ready. Understandably so. I do have an odd manner...'

She stopped him. 'No. No. And I would rather you *weren't* understanding. Why shouldn't your style…' She groped for one of *his* words. '…sequester me. Don't apologise for who you've become.'

'The stuff I read. How I see life. It's made it hard. Sure – there's the entertainment value, the quirky tremors from my tongue. But that doesn't sustain me. We all want to 'fit' with someone – be thought of as beautiful and remarkable. I know I'm laying it on here…weeks in advance of when its due, but you've fast-tracked me. I blame you entirely…'

'Would I be a throwaway accessory to you?'

'Only at weekends.'

'Don't joke.'

'OK. Never. Do you honestly see me that way? As having some kind of…*power*? You mess with me about only biting if asked. And I love that in you. To think that I would somehow want to ditch such glorious traits! It's kooky, absurd.'

They were a similar age – him one year her senior. Both just beyond the 40-sign, stuck as it was half way along the menacing road of life. He had done this before – entered a woman's domain only weeks after she had hit one of the big decades. It had probably been the last time he had dallied with freedom and a sense that things could actually happen.

What went on in a woman's head on reaching such a landmark, he wasn't entirely sure. He had been placed as a co-pilot twice now. And this new Vespa-like, hair-blowing-in-the-wind adventure buzzed with a hint of destiny.

In her he saw a caring soul and a stilettoed sumptuousness. She was testament to him needing fun again, not the dry tendrils of a pointless climb.

She held him in her gaze now. Thought about what he had transformed in her life in such a short time: the deluge of effusiveness disguised as it was by humour and the crank suggestion of a 2014 double wedding at Eastnor Castle; the paradoxical and seeming morality of his manoeuvres despite her 'Jolene' role; the honesty with which he spoke in amongst the clown-like words.

When had she last bathed in something like this without alcohol to aid her?

She asked herself, if it began to rain and he refused to move, would she stay here on this spot with him; The Hug's Club only anchor – its principal and prescient member.

'Do you know – we seem to play off each other quite well. Your situation unsettles me, but I would find it difficult to give you up.'

'I suppose I just want us to be duffers in each others' presence. That's my goal. Not impressive or put on at all. Just loose and unpolished.'

She smiled, then remembered some other words of his: "Let's meet every day. We don't even have to speak. But to see you…"

'You really are demure,' he bounded in with.

'I'm not.'

'*You are*. Behind the brazen laughter, you're a coy and modest girl.'

There was nothing she could say except to beam at him for teasing her.

'Your laughter at times stops the romance getting in, but how can I possibly ask you to curb such delight and replace it with rapture…'

There was another burst from her. Rapture was unlikely anytime soon. He remembered the photo of her (sent within days of their first exchange of letters): the large sunglasses obscuring those clever, continental eyes; the pretty blouse failing to placate her titanic, yet proportionate bust; the long, parted hair – sultry and stylish; the soft, ivory skin, especially pleasant on her – as she referred to them – "midget digits"; her bossy-looking eyebrows alert and ready to rein in or celebrate impropriety.

Too fine a specimen, he thought. Perhaps it would be better if you blew it now – were riddled with flaws – rather than turn into the perfect woman. Presently, I can just about hold it together. But, later on, if you were to throw me in the gutter…

He recalled Salinger's Dostoevsky line in his *Esme* story: "What is hell? The suffering of being unable to love." He assumed a connection with war – the fracturing of one's hopes and clarity, the dissonance raging in one's mind. What was this if not full of metallic fervour?

'Do you think I want something reckless in you?' she suddenly and quite magnificently posed.

'I hope not, although I can use a trapeze.'

It was back to the misshapen answers, his fear of appearing too ardent. Let him hear those words again: "…something reckless in you?"

He wasn't sure. Attention and affection were two very different things. Often, men fell tendering the latter.

Putting her words together, her sentences, over the last few weeks, he seemed to glean hope. The exclamation marks and artistic winks were open to ambiguity and a less secure, unfathomable expression, yet the overall mood was surely ebullient and unstinting.

He thought how she was peculiarly drawn to naivety and humour – characteristics which were tragic if left alone. Did he really have either of these? Perhaps when he spoke, people actually took his droll forlornness as wit rather than the bruising dissatisfaction which bored through him daily. And his apparent "naivety" – perhaps it bore relation to his taste; he enjoyed listening to the madcap *Just a Minute*, eating purple-sprouting broccoli, playing ping pong, watching documentaries, smelling paperback pages and women's choice of perfume as they cantered past his seat on the train.

A better use of the five senses, he could not devise. But what possible woman could suffer this?

'Are you experienced with women?'

This was it – the arching pitch. The deciding play. He sensed that she thought of him as too intelligent (and therefore not an able lover?) because he bumbled a few top-notch words. Well, he thought of her as too worldly, suspecting that she easily surpassed the paltry three partners he had slept with.

Naivety? There you have it. Sufficient to counter his immorality, he hoped.

'A long marriage would appear to suggest so, if not numerically then due to proximity, but we were hardly scampering into the biology lab every day, week or even month…'

'You stopped making love?'

'Some time ago.'

'But that's not why you want me now…'

'It isn't.'

They fell silent. Each a little sad. Each seeking flattery.

'I want you now because – and perhaps I've got this wrong – you're open with me, so brutally frank that I feel refreshed, enlivened in your company. It's the pathetic Jack Nicholson quote across from Diane Keaton: "You make me want to be a better man."'

He bowed his head. He couldn't stand the possibility of nothing coming back – her eyes perchance empty and journey-less.

She lifted his chin with her slender, majestical fingers, looked at him firmly and yet couldn't find the words.

'We should get back,' she ventured.

'Otherwise we'll both get sacked.'

'And how would we fund Eastnor then...'

'Quite.'

They both looked a shade disappointed. Neither of them wanted to be the first person to turn their back.

He saw a lunatic up in the window of her office looking down on them like a castle watchman. Do you know what you've got here? he felt like shouting. A woman whose senses haven't been drawn out, stoked or paired up. Didn't you see her quiet supplication through the bravado?

She leant forward for a kiss. He aimed for her right cheek, yet sensed her offering only a tiny part of it in order that their lips clash. He brushed them, came away with dusky fragments of her lipstick.

Was it to be? he wondered. Would he eventually crash through her sporadic private person 'façade' (her having finally seen something in him) and come away with her hand?

He knew nothing other than it wasn't his right to make demands. However much he craved her. However much it tortured him to think of her with other men. She would have to come to him. Fully. Her mind seized with possibilities.

The Pictures on the Cabinets (2012)

He vowed not to be a poor father. He vowed to take his now eight-year-old son back to the points in time where he had failed him. The excuses and blanks had come to weigh on him. His 'I don't know's had become too many. Too many for credibility. Too many to continue their father/son pact in a fruitful and trusting manner.

It had started with one. A simple question, but beyond his neurological capacity all the same. "Daaad – how do they do that? How do planes stay in the sky?" It should have been straightforward. It should have meant a mere skimming of his brain. "They have big engines and big wings" somehow decried science though, left a hole, a quizzical expression which he chose to hang and ignore rather than feed off. And such questions had started to mount, proliferate, rankle ever since.

How could he be someone he was not? How could he admit to his peers that his own schooling had been poor and thus seek their input (in the process dishing out and diluting some of his fatherhood)? He wanted the boy, *his* boy, to know he was a good source, to continue asking this and that. Not freeze, tighten up, look at his father with a modicum of shame and weariness.

He started to look for moments when his son was unusually quiet, when formerly he would have spluttered forth a barrage of questions. 'What are you thinking, Nicholas?' 'Nothing, Dad,' was the immediate response, as if inhabiting a different world, a higher calling, an esoteric plane fit for 'special ones' only.

He thought of how best to move things on, to till at the earth between them. Short of implanting a chip and dazzling his son with all manner of astounding facts, he could not take a huge leap. He would instead have to engage him with what he knew or thought – political ire, films, current affairs.

'Do you know that clowns in Spain are having to get different jobs?'

'Why would I want to know that?'

He had a feeling that the picture attached to the article – of a family stood in an agricultural field – had contributed to his son's impudence rather than the story itself. High unemployment, despondency and shifting vocations were hardly attention grabbers. Better to have a painted face with a huge frown.

He searched for more stories from his weekly read. The father of Donkey Kong, Shigeru Miyamoto was still working three decades on. He looked at Nicholas's electronic gadget and realised the connection. Same manufacturer. Miyamoto appeared to be a happy man, with his black, floppy hair greying slightly and his impressive white teeth signalling a youth never quite conceded. Even his skin – surely susceptible in such a job – looked radiant.

He was the embodiment of contentment – something which had hurdled Nicholas's father again and again. Which bit then – which part of this article should he show his son.

'You can compare Miyamoto with Balzac in terms of output. Slightly more than one game for every novel.'

'Soooooo....'

'Do you know, Nicholas that before he designed some of the games you have cartridges for, he was responsible for the pictures on the cabinets in the amusement arcades. What does that tell you?'

'Where was the first amusement arcade?'

'I don't know, but that wasn't...' He gave up. Children could be discursive. It made his inner turmoil boil less, yet could not completely quash a feeling of inadequacy. His mind had departed significantly in recent years – to an emptiness, a procedural hell, an epoch of suspension between youth and retirement. On one occasion, he had considered boarding school for his son, such was the disappointment in himself, his inability to master the world in a tangible and satisfactory way. Why risk the next generation struggling also? That is what he thought. Despite the pain Nicholas's absence would bring. Irrespective of damaged future relations. One day perhaps Nicholas would begin to understand his father's well-intentioned goodness, his realism, stung as it was by fearfulness.

Now though, there was an effort less desperate and defeatist. Into focus came the questions which had been shunted aside. 'The Gunpowder Plot. 1605. You asked me who wrote the anonymous letter to Lord Monteagle, tipping him off.'

'Yes. But we've moved on to other things.'

'Still. I'd like to tell you.'

'Do you have to…'

'Francis Tresham. It was Francis Tresham – Monteagle's brother-in-law.'

'Right.'

Somehow, the intervening eighteen months had dampened his son's enthusiasm. Understandably, he thought. He should have acted at the time. When he needed it. Displayed a teacherly zest. Instead…what had happened? Could he trace each lost moment, lost chance, to being busy, distracted, tired and incapable?

He looked at his son from afar with renewed vigour. Had he tainted their special bond through neglect? Had he not quite realised what he was doing? (The slow burn of disenfranchisement – his boy's privileges and rights to answers sacrificed at the altar of the soporific and inadequate.) He needed to understand that he himself was a lost cause yet that did not, should not, prevent him striving for others.

Pride no longer belonged at his core. Shame was to take the wheel and announce the potential of his son to the world. Give up. He was to give up any sense that he could achieve things – revel in glory of any kind. He should instead act as a mere vehicle for his son's wants and dreams. Coalesce possibility and achievement.

Not long ago – before Nicholas's consciousness had grown exponentially – he had made a point of always leaving doors open. Between their two bedrooms. Between the kitchen and the garden. Why? Because his son's pain had to be his. Sickness and accidents had to be listened out for, rushed upon and healed by whatever method. Perhaps he had let such attention slide. Perhaps the precocious, mental behemoth at the side of him had duped him into thinking he was fit to travel alone. When in fact, it was the father's presence that had allowed intelligence and security to blossom simultaneously.

'You used to mention the stars a lot more. You were fascinated. We talked of getting an observatory.'

'I think I stopped looking up.'

'Life can do that to us. We can all build on our interest in the skies with what Pythagoras and Copernicus knew though.'

'Our teachers tell us to dive in – discover things for ourselves. When did you last…'

Nicholas saw the expression on his father's face. He hadn't 'dived in' to anything for years and so what could he say in response? Nicholas had once asked "How do you understand things, Dad?" To that he had an answer: "Context." But now, to feign passion, urgency, the ability to be brave. He simply couldn't lie.

'It's been a while, son. I'm trying to get back on that track. Perhaps together…'

'Yes.' Nicholas wasn't sure if he meant it or not, but the open grieving had pulled the affirmative out of him.

'Would you like to go to the airport and watch the planes take off one day?'

Still hesitation, a lack of resoluteness. Nicholas wasn't sure if a father was meant to operate this way. His friends' dads simply swept them up, told them how it was going to be.

'I don't know anybody that does that. Why not *go somewhere* while you're there?'

'People couldn't always afford to.'

'Can we?'

'Not really.'

'Oh.'

It – their relationship – felt slightly derelict, death-like. As if there were no more cards to play. Surely, if he trawled through their father/son archive there would be something, an 'I don't know' he could resurrect, turn on its head. He thought, wondered if he was much, much worse than the other fathers. Is not knowing, not having the capacity really so bad, or was it that he had started to put possible embarrassment (a reluctance in public) before his son's growth?

Of this, he knew he was guilty. Particularly as he watched other fathers who were less guarded, less chiding when it came to their children's wildness. The unpredictable elements in Nicholas were proving to be difficult. The grand plan – chess one day, football the next, discussions about film and politics the rest of the time – had fallen early; never really shown promise of any kind. Children's lives were so...blighted by current trends, cultures around them, that parental nurture had become a dream, an unrealistic baron in fancy dress.

People took Nicholas to restaurants his father didn't approve of. Places where cheap, Chinese toys were dished out as a form of fleeting gratification. And these people were close relations – Nicholas's mother, grandparents. Poor cultural ambassadors who laughed in his face and claimed he was denying Nicholas a real childhood.

How? he asked himself. By steering him away from the smallness of life? By not giving in to the popular forces around him? He had never purported to be intelligent but he would not stand by while modern day Ostrogoths shepherded his child to scabrous dens.

He had seen inside these grease pits with their Formica tables and tempting wall colours. They were magnets for embryonic and malleable minds, dancing buildings of non-nutrition and postponed sickness.

He thought once of running in with a fake machine gun – scaring the burgers out of the hands of unknowing diners. "Just what is it you're doing?!" he would shout. They would look dumbfounded. Be unable to grasp his central premise. More vitriolic lines would follow. "This!" He would point all around the lowbrow restaurant. "Sitting here. Turning your kid into a junkie." Nothing would come back. Just the ketchup-splattered faces of the tiny brigade before him.

Settling down, he realised he might lose Nicholas even if he kept him. There was no way of blocking the malevolent forces. Moments *did* prevail – tiny breakthroughs – but he wasn't the man he expected to be. Fatherhood had somehow been a brief reign – over in six or seven years. Because now, Nicholas had wit and at least a *scattered* and quixotic certainty.

There had once been the question about white rail-track boxes. What do they do? What are they for? Nicholas had noticed them a few feet apart, just above the track, only at station platforms.

'Is that the highest the snow can go, Dad?'

'I don't think so. Not sure what they're for. Let me find out for you.'

And he had. Not immediately. But after a little tentative shuffling. Making sure no one was in the station queue. And then excusing his 'daft question' through the glass screen.

It had taken three attempts. The ticket staff were not often the brightest. The chubby aficionado who he knew used to spot came out from behind his desk, through the side door and onto the platform. Angling his body, rather than squatting down, he spoke carefully: "Datum plates, sir. They monitor movement in the track. The red slider block is generally 300 millimetres above the rail head. A green block and re-alignment is needed."

He thanked him. Noticed the absence of green blocks along the platform wall. Told Nicholas the story. It had been one of the few times his son had looked intrigued. Something to stir those neglected brain cells. A technical piste for him to slalom down. But since then...very little. He supposed that Nicholas wanted more natural answers, a flow of words that unveiled a suitable path.

What could this man possibly offer him? It was dangerous that they were still together. Dangerous for the country that he was being held back. Perhaps prevented from getting into engineering, medicine, law. Like mixing brimstone with something bromidic.

Nicholas's father remembered the kids from his own childhood: Holden (Management Consultant); Smith (Accountant); Grayson (Greenkeeper); Onley (Navy). They had moved on. All of them. Even Grayson, who knew about grass. He examined himself. Office man. What did he actually know? How to acquiesce, grovel. Was it even a profession? Could he sit in a pub now with these people and not be appalled at what he had amounted to?

Once, not too many years ago, he had been a funny man, an observer of life, had had people rolling about at funerals. (Not at all conscious of the dwindling timeframe before him.) Life had seemed almost *too* easy, manageable, void of responsibility. Now, however – unlike when Nicholas was born – there seemed to be a drag, something pulling him back. Mainly because there was nothing to move forward to. No world that he liked. No offer of sustenance. No mould within which his values could be stored.

He looked at his son. And then held him. Tighter than normal as he was readying him for bed. The pyjamas had coloured robots on. They were suggestive of play, excitement, wonder; all of the things he had lost and would be unable to spark in his child. Someone had once told him "Life is one big scrap but be sure to leave something beautiful behind". Well, he was doing that. In the morning he wouldn't be there. And to the tragic question his boy might ask – *Where's* Daddy? – could only be the sullied words: 'I don't know.'

Modest Anger (2009)

He thought it possible to continue his dalliances and exchanges in life without the merciless directness that imbued most others. In his friends he placed a covenant, a mutually acceptable deal, which savoured extra politeness. They would walk together, saunter and instantly know where the boundaries lay; why their conversation needed to sail above the lower ilk.

On this day, however, Roddy broke rank – filled the air with a pungent expression: 'You'd like to fuck her...really catalogue her finest parts.'

'I...I'd...certainly enjoy her company,' Tom replied, disappointed by the easy blasphemy, the pitiful lapse. He surveyed his friend, ran the rule over him. You've killed the enigma of what we're striving for, he thought. Speaking really is easy, but speaking with grace a different matter. I thought you were one of the few, but different, opposing bits of you I keep on seeing. Why *not* speak like this? People tell me that I'm a century behind, but what are *they* exactly...exhibitionists, cheap language purveyors.

Roddy was irked by the tame response, yet forgave his companion, allowed the sentence to pass without fuss. 'What if that's your downfall? That modern woman no longer seeks courtesy and beating around the bush?'

'I'm hoping she's not modern,' Tom replied, disappointed, unable to look his friend in the face. Why the devil's advocate all of a sudden? he thought. Has our usual support and camaraderie for one another left you worn out, bored even? He examined his friend's gangly frame. How easily respect turned into resentment. How you thought you were with a fellow who largely shared your world view, only to be let down, bamboozled one might say.

Tom felt like cursing him. What do you know of *my* woman?! Take a look at your own – the one who shouts at you, throws things, has you tethered and bound. And your character beyond that – quick to suggest a different career for me when you yourself despise what you do and yet remain…king of the procrastinators. You do not know what is good for my heart strings, nor do you know which job I am suited to!

'I think all women sip from the tank of modernity to a degree. Would prefer an automatic door rather than one held open for them.'

You think your mutterings splendid! You think them astute somehow when all I see are generalisations. Lost in your expression is the belief that originality can survive, that the popular rakings of the majority are nothing more than paltry attempts at leading the way.

'We are clerks, are we not, Roddy. I forget how we started these tête-à-têtes, what exactly drew us together, made us conspire, but is it not the ordinariness of our working lives which stands as a warning against folly and idiocy? Some of what you have said of late I have found not to be in keeping with our usual high standards...'

'And some of what you've said I've found to be dreamy, quixotic. I well remember the seeds of our collaboration – it was when I lifted up my keyboard and threw it against the desk. In that act, you saw nihilism instead of frustration I now venture. You had me down for a misanthrope yet there are many things I love.'

'I had you down as someone who would share in a person's disquiet if they showed an understanding of your own. How wrong I was...'

'And this because – remind me – I do not see one naïve and beautifully-draped woman...ready to be lifted, inspired, shown a world which stands apart from that which we inhabit?'

'Yes. And because you lack hope.'

'Superstition, I think you mean.'

'You would do that? Bundle all my graceful thoughts together and label them irrational? Hard to believe we tolerated each other for so long.'

They stopped. Could no longer walk side by side. 'Choose a direction, sir.'

'This,' Tom replied, refusing to switch his footing.

'Very well.' Roddy about-faced, was surprised somewhat by the conviction of his erstwhile friend.

They strode apart, almost like the beginnings of a duel. It was too much for Tom to leave at the word 'well' though. Things were far from well. 'You refuse to believe there's at least one woman who has repudiated all the bogus customs placed upon her! You have given up and expect all others to follow suit!'

Roddy turned, ran in his direction, immediately pointed a finger at him. 'You want some dumb fuck of a woman to be grateful for your attention – that's what this amounts to. You want her to stare up into your eyes and worship your pseudo-originality.'

'No. That's not it. I merely want her to believe in the divine.'

'Yes. *Your* supreme worth.'

'What makes you draw such a conclusion? What have you seen in me that leads you to think that I need such flattery?'

'You delude yourself. Whether out of ignorance or a preferred path, I don't know. But you like to invent angelic characteristics in a person and the flip side of that is you expect reciprocation. Often, I think, it's because you cannot handle a stain on your personality. That if someone were to point out your flaws, you'd cease to exist rather than accept that some of you is bad.'

'No. No. Nonsense. Absolute nonsense. Be on your way again if that is the only reasoning you have.'

'We're all bad, Tommy. Accept it! What you're seeking is either a self-oppressor or a blind woman unaware of life's evils.'

'You think I oppress...what – myself?'

'Yes. I do. And have thought it for a while. You want things too clean...unruffled.'

'I...I want someone not caught up in it. The stampede. The 'progression'.'

'You want an uneconomic bean head.'

'What is that exactly?'

'I don't know, but she doesn't exist I tell you. And any woman will resent you if you place that on her...order her to hold back. Unlearn.'

Tom shook his head. Walked away. He didn't want any of that. But merely someone who paused. Took stock of life. Ideally *she* would find *him*. Perhaps stalk him. Interestingly enough, such a prospect didn't concern him. How enlivening to be noticed! How…he didn't know.

Suddenly suspended, he felt. As if there was no one now. Neither his parents, nor a set of companions. Things were *not* earned, he attested, but greased over. He had never felt utterly comfortable in Roddy's presence. He hated his old man clothes, his coffee-stained teeth, his gaunt, multiplex face. And the agreeing with him for so long – almost reversing their ages. Why had he subjugated his finer ideas to this lesser man's generalised hotchpotch – the thickening of which was only possible due to it having *him* as its audience?

Who was Roddy? Someone so damn sure and yet open to only popular insights. They would interact like an uncle and nephew at times; Tom barricaded in by the man's inveterate obstinance, his 'quick to damn' non-educational quotes. Are we different because of our degrees? thought Tom. I, the English man, Roddy environmental. No. It cannot be so. There were plenty of dopes, stragglers and supercilious types doing English. What distinguishes us then? I must find out.

He went home. To his modest terraced. Roddy had the girl – a sometime nutcase – but not the house. Tom could at least move around – not have the misfortune of staring at his parents each evening. Perhaps this had hardened Roddy – his missing the property ladder. Made him not believe in anything anymore. No recreational den – no natural growth. A portrayal of maturity only. Inhibited at every turn and then a free run at work, a chance to *attempt* to be who he thought he was.

Perhaps Tom needed to pity him, show tact, quietly afford him the upper hand. They occasionally laughed after all. About what, he tried to remember. It was a kind of toff laughter – demeaning not in a foul or pernicious sense, but one which cradled a literary existence. And there was the irony. Roddy aspired to a finer life – books, art, theatre – but was often quite heartless; his sentences far from subtle. There was a callous disregard at times. When they playfully mocked their own anger – concluded at the end of each lunch session whether today's tone had been self-pitying, misogynistic or delightfully political – Tom was always disturbed by his friend's hypocrisy.

'You should move over to this side of the business. You should understand why management speaks the way it does.'

'Whatever happened to unqualified anger?!' Tom had slung back at him one day. 'Ridiculous assumptions based on nothing more than sketchy insights...'

Roddy had actually come over to his side at this point. By then, Tom had dismissed him as too serious a man though. Something he himself obviously was. The common ground had thus become a mirror with a multitude of light, a turgid reminder of one's less graceful characteristics. Each of them stared into the other and resented the thing coming back.

If I am to have a woman, Tom thought, then I cannot possibly show her Roddy. I would rather not show her anyone, but Roddy in particular would infect her, seize her expression and disfigure it. Yes, there was charm – an honest graft – but it melted once you knew him. Sneak away – don't we all want to do this with Miss Perfect. Sit opposite each other in a fire-lit room and then just jump – attack the lips, feel young again, lessen the love algorithm that seems to have grown too complex over the years.

Meeting her. He knew where she stood. What he had to do. How to sequester her angled grace. To many she was ordinary, not at all beautiful or striking, but rather fusty, too talkative, bland. Tom saw in her, however, first of all the red hair – or more crucially the personality it fostered. She exuded a kindliness, an unimposing needfulness. After a date or two you would be utterly hers. She was desirous of someone with purpose, real integrity – a man with perhaps only a fitful optimism, a man who could be in cahoots with her. They each wanted to turn to someone in any situation and know...simply know that a gym mat was there to cushion the fall.

He had talked to her once previously – twice if you included his indicating that the recently vacated train seat was to be hers; a woman – a much needier and deserving cause than his own 'beastly' agenda. She had been appreciative of this. There was none of the automatic assumption that befell so many women these days, none of the rude aggression. This immediately endeared her to him, her glinting eyes occasionally looking up, assimilating the architect of this simple gesture but overwhelming generosity all the same.

She was a woman who still had room for politeness – did not wish to negotiate it away at the feminist altar. Tom remembered the one occasion he had sat next to her. The button had flown off her coat and leapt over him into the aisle. He had fortunately located its landing spot and passed it back to her. She laughed at the spectacle – gratefully took the button from between his fingers. Her attention was complete, even in instances like this. You were with her and twenty others this side of the carriage and yet...somehow transported, isolated from the rest. Their conversation had been so innocent yet absolute. Full of imparted giggles and amusement. As he got off, he wished her good luck in finding a suitably coloured thread – something that had mildly troubled her but only in an 'excuse to talk' fashion.

He always turned, looked in the window as the train departed. Never quite seeing her, he often considered driving to her stop four stations on. No. What would that achieve...except nervousness, suspicion. The popular press had seen to it that romance was now part of the stalker's canon. Anything not predictable with an unknown person was a sign to flee, scarper, scream in need of a vigilante huddle.

Once he had her, it would be enough. Tom was not a man's man, but rather an observer of life. He required neither the five fingers of respect nor camaraderie in its various forms. He could be direct, but only with himself through the thoughts that were a bubble bath to his mind. Often walking behind her for instance, he wondered what it would be like to lift her skirt, unclip her stockings and push her through an imaginary door. Sharing this, as he had attempted to do infrequently over the years, had merely resulted in a dangerous concoction, or the embarrassing and false notion that he was still effeminate in his expression. Best to keep quiet. Accept that resentments often grew when you stood at the border of office talk. Yet think! – these people, at some point, were alone and then, only then, would they understand your methods.

If Roddy ever met her – which Tom would strenuously attempt to re-route or detour – then there should not be laughter. A stifled exchange – yes. A comfortable, political openness – yes. But laughter – no. It would act as an incubator to future meetings, as a lynchpin to respect. And Tom's girl was not to respect Roddy. She was to trust his own health warnings on the matter, understand that a deed had taken place that had unsettled Tom.

When? When do I ask her out? he quizzed himself. Not Monday, because the day is peculiar. Not Tuesday or Wednesday because such days store up possible heartache for the rest of the week. Thursday? Yes – Thursday. Time to mourn before the weekend if the plan fails. He set the date in his mind. Would save his finest shirt for the occasion. Unsure though. Whether to pull her to one side before the busy descent down the steps onto the platform. Or casually nestle himself next to her two minutes before the train's arrival.

He left it to the day. Fate. The flow of people. An unsullied remark would perhaps start them off – an introductory line versed in candour and sweetness. Did they not kind of know each other already? Hadn't their small exchange of words represented a beginning? Too many past errors of judgement left Tom unsure. Where did politeness end and the angels' choir lend itself to a conductor? Maybe it wasn't the rejections that beseeched him but his susceptibility, his thin skin. Didn't others move on with a shrug of the shoulders if their target rebuffed them? Tom planned ahead too far – allowed them to rip out not simply a first date but a joint-named mortgage. Quite ridiculous, he thought to himself. I should tame my imagination.

The day came. His breathing was tangible almost. His footwork tentative. He knew a little about her – separated, one son – from conversations he had overheard between her and a female friend. These facts augmented what little belief he had. Do you know, he thought – I somehow stopped growing at thirty. Where others have hues of knowing and tentacles of absolute confidence (even if misguided), I have diffidence…the desire to lie low.

There. Now. He went against his natural reservedness – tailed her up the steps. Following the calves, the coat, the red hair, he saw in her someone a little like him. No one had ever really whooped about her, told her she was incredible, daunting in a non-glitzy fashion, insisted that she deserved to be worshipped.

Tom took his customary two steps at a time up the passage – remained barely three feet away from her. How her face needed to be touched. How her arms needed shifting into the pose of a classical dancer. His mind raced away. His heart pumped the blood around him even faster. His shoe angled itself quite awkwardly against the step now in front of him. 'Shhii…'

He tumbled – careered towards the Ls in front of him. His right knee took the full force of the gradient's harsh stolidness. 'Aaahh!' The commotion, the ferment, was enough to warrant a few calls of concern around him. 'Nasty.' 'Oooh. Are you OK?' 'Let me help you up…'

He generously assisted whoever it was handling him by motioning upwards – relieving them of his weight. 'Thank you,' he ennobled him/her with. But then…his eyes traced the heels, the stockings, the winter coat. Her. It was her. She had come *to him*. Serendipity! Hallelujah!

'A rather large button has fallen this time,' she seemed to serenade him with. Tom – injured, bruised – simply laughed. He would let her nurse him, sit him down in a quiet corner. They would both miss the train, but joy would embrace them. Its cousin, exultation, would...

He sat up. She was gone. Tomorrow. Yes – tomorrow. Definitely.

Liar (2010)

He came home one night in the eleventh year of his employment with the firm and realised that he was a liar. Not in a terribly bad sense, he thought. But…a liar all the same. Prone to changing the temperature of a sentence. Prone to giving himself a safety net no matter what. Small things really. Subtle ways of strengthening his hand. A 'No. Not at all' for a 'Yes.' A laugh instead of frankness; the bolder option capable of messing up his day. Simple avoidance of, well, controversy.

He knew there were richer fruits once past the grapple, the initial struggle of forthrightness, but, no – he couldn't bear it.

He settled down with a straight-forward tea – sliced potatoes roasted, steamed carrots and broccoli, cod bathed in lemon. The radio was always on when he ate. It was his partner at the table, his speech maker and confidante. When he listened attentively, he dreamed of better things – maybe working in the media himself, perhaps offering the world the side of him which (through necessity, he thought) was blackened out.

Now. Now though. When you see absolutely what you have become. What then? He got up, brushed the tiny remains from his plate into the bin and stacked the crockery neatly. Ready for its swim. Ready for its daily ritual.

Here at least is truth, he thought – never buying a dishwasher. Staring out onto the back lawn whilst partaking in this honest and thorough cleansing. A weight removed. In the slow, methodical canter of washing up something transcendental occurred. The world slowed. Routine and thought came together. Such a state could not last though. Once everything was spotless he would look around for a similar chore. Be disturbed by the void, the vacuum. His thoughts would turn to the processes at work and such analysis was wretched (somehow). It broke him. To know that their cloak was firmly against his skin.

He paced the house. Needed to inhabit a form of karma, run with rhythm of a certain kind. The waste, he thought. Of his evenings. Never mapping out his route back to idealism. He did not wish to think too deeply of his plight – that was the problem. Instead, he would bathe it in alcohol and current affairs. Lie. Yes, lie to his shaken and pitiful frame.

'Why? Why don't you look the bad ones in the eye?' he muttered. 'Make them at least know that other, confident opinions exist. No,' he damned/lambasted himself – 'You shelve such simplicity…stare down at the rotten floor, afford their baseless direction a comfy acquiescence.'

Not liking himself, he had placed rectangular bits of paper around the house – each one with those four letters on them: L I A R. It became a mnemonic. He would think of ways to berate his sodden frame.

'You Little Idiotic Ass-licking Reprobate. Lunatic In A Rumpus. Laughed-at Island Arraigned by Repugnance.'

After consuming his fourth wine he tore such criticism down – screwed the bits of paper into a giant ball, but could not conjure up the energy to walk to the bin. 'Damn it! Damn it! Where is this heading? What do I have left?'

He thought how when he was twenty that death at eighty seemed like a short life. Now, half way there, however, and he wondered in his current state how he could possibly make it. Once the cloak of lies was placed around your shoulders, something happened. You became complicit. Dirty. Part of an ugly fellowship. You were supposed to let things slide. Alter your moral compass. Be in tune with how money was *really* made.

'No! I cannot do it!' he screamed. 'I can no longer nod my head instead of shaking it. I will go in. Tell them how it is.'

He slept fine. Better than normal in fact. The phoniness that had dogged him for years felt, all of a sudden, weightless – quite feather-like. His breakfast tasted sublime, extraordinary even. The cut of his clothes seemed to be exquisite despite his out-of-shape torso. It was as if he had released a million endorphins. Collaborated with Mandela and Luther King Jr. Spontaneously learnt to become strong, yet welcoming.

On the train into work there was no anxiousness, no picking at his shameful and sullied existence. Merely depth and radiance now. He stared out of the window and was met with an extra light, a quite becoming and subtle communication with God.

Why didn't you show me this before? he asked the light. Why hide one's abilities and conviction? No answer came back. God had clearly rushed to another appointment.

He stepped off the train, walked down the gangplank and column and eventually found himself on the pavement just three hundred metres from work. Crossing the road, he noticed the new posters in their plastic, rectangular homes. Culture. Art. Humour. Museums. The latter, in particular, grabbed him: *Shaped by War* was the heading above a weary, trench-tanned individual in full army getup. The stare was meaningful, somehow greater than the actuality of his existence. Years of hell for this? A dark, sorrowful snap bathed in the appreciation of later generations.

He thought how *he* was shaped. By bastards no doubt. Singularly focused 'leaders' unwilling to discuss policy and decision-making. To be under these for much longer – Christ!

The walk became heavier. Now he planned to challenge them, shift his head above the parapet, his initial few minutes in the 'prison', the carpeted station would be hard. Rebels or subversives tended to be rounded up like lone Indians – receive the full barracking and outrage of an ignorant class. Don't you understand colonialism?! Don't you play by team rules?! Selfish! You are selfish!! And the ones who understood his motives, his frantic and isolated salvo, remained mute. Unable to help his cause because of their own predicaments, financial dependence and the age-old burden of 'expectation'.

Pushing his weight against the horrible revolving door, this gadget of right-wing encouragement, he thought how some people were quite rough with this spinning ingress, routinely savage and unfeeling in their 'thrust', their momentum-creating push. In these people, he recognised 'fine company attributes', a hunger to succeed, a frothing keenness, a willingness to surpass small concerns.

How did I fall to such a level? he thought. Surrounded by mercenaries. Buffeted by corporate winds. Good god. Is this to be my final calling? Will I have a heart attack here and my shirt unbuttoned by a person I hate? Will they feign concern and crank up a few points for the company? If these bastards even step into the crematorium building (thus attend my send-off), I will be apoplectic. I will conjure up a hurricane which only the worthy can escape. To the coddling hypocrites that loiter around my ashen frame, I say to you: Be off! Gain your glee elsewhere.

He made it to the thick, fire proof door after climbing one set of steps. There was a narrow, rectangular window through which he could view the prosaic activities. Same old, same old, he exasperatingly muttered. Death by office work! The younger ones unwitting victims of a contemporary tragedy.

Entering the floor – which was half a football pitch in size – he refused to be cosseted by kindness or pleasantries. Suspicion and scepticism were to play a hand in all his exchanges now, bar two (friends who had proven themselves during lunchtime strolls). Reaching his part of the office, he stalled briefly – looked at his colleagues with a degree of mystification.

'This isn't a family,' he spoke, rather louder than planned. 'It's a mockery.'

'A mockery?' his immediate boss asked.

'Yes.'

'Of what?'

Time. Time to hit them. Go full throttle with this carefully constructed theory. Alter not just his life, but a small portion of theirs. 'Of...'

He would be poor if he saw it through. Banished from an industry which he didn't find taxing, but merely disheartening. Merely? He was lying again. It was insufferable. A slow, fathomless existence before he dropped off his perch. Uninteresting. A non-stimulant if ever there was one. A killer. A brutal if understated remedy for life. A means of throwing one's education up in the air because three types of people rose: the uninquisitive; the cock-suckers; and the sycophants. Their very own UCAS clearing system!

'Of no-holds barred, intelligent interaction.'

His boss walked up to him in an effort to quell or make private the conversation. 'You know – sometimes there are things you do which we don't approve of but let go. We do that because we know you're an asset. Is that what you're referring to but hidden from your radar?'

He was ready for this moment. Not unduly put off by the buttering up, the sweet-sounding but rehearsed riposte. 'No. No, it's not. It's much larger than that. Subtle warnings over the years have made me conscious of when and when not to speak. You've politicised my expression which I see as very harmful. What is worse, you continue with rhetoric which suggests the contrary of 'our' firm. Perhaps I should be ashamed that I do not understand the game or wish to be dressed by it. Perhaps my self-imposed exile away from sophistication and professionalism is to be scorned. The odd thing is that I still see pockets of candidness in various industries and they are the examples I wish to follow.'

'You're not suggesting...surely after spending a large part of your career here, you wouldn't just up sticks. Principle is all well and good, but...'

'But?'

'Can we sit down and discuss this properly?'

He didn't want to, however, something in him acceded to the request. Behind closed doors, in one of the tiny offices, he would become more vociferous, vehement – one of them.

'A drink?'

'No. No. Just the conversation.'

'OK. Can I say that other members of the team have been in this situation. Stir crazy from years in the same job. Desperate to taste something new...'

'This isn't about the 'new' though. I'm not a man of change. I simply want to speak my mind.'

'There are sessions for that. We can increase them.'

'Sessions?! As if we were born to lie with truth as a luxury. I'm not built for such a system.'

'You must know that history's a lie – that the victors write it?'

'It depends where you look. Whether you're a surface man, whether you trust Fleet Street's rags.'

'Then you don't? And you think us so different?'

'I wouldn't pretend to know you. Only judge what you do and how you speak to others.'

'I don't inspire you?'

'No.'

'Why ever not?'

'You're not political enough.'

'You've obviously never seen me across the table from my father.'

'Tory Vs Tory. Not quite politics. More dividing up the ill-gotten gains.'

'You think I'm like that?'

'Please tell me otherwise...'

'I can't.'

'Well then.'

'And you'd rather not work under a Tory?'

'No. I'd rather not continue to allow my brain cells to die.'

'Promotion then...It's...'

'A terrible route.'

'You seem quick to draw such a conclusion.'

'I see the people that rise…'

'And?'

'They…are different to me.'

'Politely put. But how?'

'They get excited. Whereas I don't.'

'Courses change that.'

'No. No. No. I'm a recalcitrant old dog. Impossible to manipulate.'

'You really see it as manipulation?'

'Yes. Gene-bending, DNA-twisting. All in all an erosion of the mind's true state.'

'You know this without going on the courses?'

'I see the clones that you rear. The disinfectants that they roll around in. I'm quite happy with what I stand for.'

'Which is what?'

'I'll tell you what it's not.'

'Go on.'

'Profit-driven. Vacuous. Light. Meaningless. Shoddy. Uninspiring.'

'A bold statement.'

'It has to be.'

'So you bluffed and lied for 10 years?'

'In part.'

'And now it's time to move on?'

'Yes.'

'Because a decade's significant? A warning shot? A huge clanging bell?'

'Something along those lines.'

'Room for another?'

'You wouldn't want the uncertainty.'

'Indeed.'

'So we're done...'

'I'd still rather not lose you.'

'It has to be. I do not like what I do.'

'Do any of us?'

'You should.'

'Really? Isn't that idealism? There are things to numb the pain.'

'I'll stick with the natural.'

He watched his boss ponder things, nod, then ponder again. He hadn't expected this. A fight of sorts. One aimed at keeping him. Nothing acrimonious. Just…everything the job hadn't been. The rack can do strange things to people. He knew it would be a hindrance hiring someone to replace him. Knew that his reliability and accuracy, if nothing else, were deemed invaluable. But life needed to move him on. He wouldn't miss them because he needed other voices in his life – one's less stale, full of genuine vigour.

There weren't many handshakes. But then, only a liar offers his palm to all, he thought.

Beg (2012)

Could it be? This man with the paper cup in his hand, sat on the pavement, motionless to the world, save a glance up at the passers-by had attended lectures and seminars with me?

The large eyes. Conspicuously the same. Impressionable and completely without ambition. The thick chops, pale yet with stubble. The coat, puffer-like, apt, suitable for this freezing weather.

How? How though had it come to this? I knew of the death of his mother some six years ago. Left to him was the house. But how had he squandered such a jewel, a gift, such inheritance?

I daren't speak to him. I know he hasn't noticed me and so I initially walk on. I am busy today. At work. Working. It is a means of paying the bills. This saunter around the city is meant to reinvigorate me – remove the weight from my mind. But this. Now. How can I possibly ignore it?

I stop. Look back. He is miserable. Christ – where has my heart gone? Why am I even hesitating, I ask myself. To get involved is to commit. Time. Emotion. A sense of belonging. I will be late back to work. Undoubtedly so. And all excuses are frowned upon nowadays. Death. Children. Sickness. Accidents.

A friend who has become homeless. How about that? Does it better the time when I lifted a deceased cat to the side of the road and consequently missed my normal train? Perhaps the owner's appreciation held no merit upon me phoning her. Perhaps I should have allowed the wounded and 'rigor mortis' animal to be driven over again and again – turned into mush or rather flattened into the road like a hedgehog.

Don't do this. We are near the end of a project. It is a critical time. What? What should I do? I should kneel down. Without delay. Without too much thought. If I was a woman I would be there now. With the right words. I would cajole other people into helping. I would immediately take you to a coffee house and talk things through.

What do I remember of him? The most striking fact is that he didn't graduate. Two years only. In the final autumn, seen asleep on a train, travelling to the north east of England. Why? I don't fully know but people talked of the pressure getting to him. His untidy mind failing to map out his dissertation. And that having a domino effect on his other courses.

His name? You wish to know his name? Simon. A kind individual. Not the brightest, but decided to major in politics. Perhaps that was his undoing. In a moment of high confidence he talked of 'academia'. People mocked his highfalutin ways. They laughed at his attempted transition into well-spoken circles.

He was always going to fail, we can now observe. Whether in love or work. He once lay on the floor while I curled up in the single bed of a Welsh girl's at university. He took to politics because the abstract and metaphorical greatness of English eluded him. He craved friendship yet did not understand its subtleties away from direct discourse. I would never have wished life become so simple for him though. Reduced to holding out a cup, wherein pity is placed.

And yet what can I say? When I saw him last and learnt of his mother's passing, he professed to me that he was a portrait artist. The pay was uneven. Most of his work was in hospitals. But, yes, he drew faces. Perhaps morphed the sick into a gallery of politicians still fresh in his head.

I didn't have many questions for him when I saw him. There was always a keenness in him which felt out of place, which unsettled me. He was so absolutely off the chart even then – full of a two-dimensional grin – that it prompted me to examine my own life. Had I got lucky? Did I simply know what to say in given situations? Or was I propping up a deceitful world?

I certainly had no concept of the world now before me. The closest I had got was waiting for a friend who *always* gave to the homeless – 50p, £1, something, enough to salvage his soul or brighten the faces lower than his own. I was scared to give. Frugal also. I had two direct debits set up with animal welfare charities. Quite a clean exchange of sorts. But people? Weren't they supposed to help themselves?

Simon so obviously hadn't. And my finer principles – born only recently – were tugging at me, asking that I engage with him. Hey, old pal – what became of you? My words would have to be better than that. Fit together. Express a warmth and buoyancy.

I looked back at him – his addled frame. This wasn't easy. I was still self-conscious despite reaching forty years of age. Whatever I say will be picked apart by the people stood around. They will examine me, wonder at my motives, snatch my words into their ears. Is he trying to bludgeon this poor man, steal from him? The worst, the very worst, the egregious played itself in my mind as to what they thought. I had the slow, suspicious movements of a bounder. I was a rip-off merchant and mugger of tramps. Unfortunate souls ought to steer clear of me.

I made my way back. Stood over him. Wished to confirm his identity. Simon. The naïve grandmaster. He didn't, at first, look up. As if by doing so, I would administer a kick to his face. Slowly though, meekly, his eyes drew themselves up to mine. Shame immediately covered him. He knew it was me – Gerard, his old buddy. His thoughts, I guessed, turned to a happier time. Unable to speak, there appeared to be an avalanche, a crumbling of his face. His head dropped and tears began to wet his cheeks.

'Go away please,' I heard him mumble. I felt stupid, a fetid reminder of his stable past. Dressed in my suit against his weather-worn and shabby attire, I looked like a rent collector. To walk away though, to allow our current, contrasting plights a dominant hold, would be to neglect his welfare, suffocate struggle instead of supporting it.

'How can I? We shared something. You were the first person at university to offer his hand to me.'

'The past has gone.'

'I don't believe that. Your dad – does he know?'

'We don't speak.'

'Simon – Christ. Let me take you somewhere.'

'No....I can't do....the normal things anymore.'

'But you must be cold, desperate for the indoors.'

He didn't answer. He had to shut me out. I was opening up wounds and to comprehend how his life had gone would be unbearable. His peers were now other homeless people alongside whom his existence seemed ok.

He stared at the pavement. His face appeared leaden and forlorn. To me he represented all that was wrong with society. We let people fall and do not pick them up. What heartless fuckers we are. Always craving the next pound but forgetting why we are here.

I didn't want to be like that. I didn't want to leave a legacy of callousness. The selfish altruists – that is what they were called. A title bestowed upon helpers. And I now understood it. There *is* an element of selfish in the selfless in that it enriches you, makes you feel at one again. I had to swerve the initial reticence of Simon and show him this was not a masquerade. His plight stripped me of dignity – the pathetic standards which we adhere to in polite exchange. With him I would have to find my old self – the one with less manners but someone more real and grounded.

'I'm packing your stuff. You're not staying out here.'

'Get…your damn paws off.'

'This isn't what was intended for you. I might not see you again.'

'Gerard – walk on.'

'No.'

'You have a job. Go to it.'

'Not until…'

'What? I'm washed? Presentable? And after that? Are you my new dad – the dad that didn't make it to my mum's funeral?'

I knelt. Leaned in. We had to find something solid to sustain us. 'I've eaten with you maybe a hundred times in the Student Union building. I've stayed over at yours numerous Thursdays. You've met my parents who couldn't believe I'd made it to university. Sure – we studied different things later on, but you made the experience welcoming for me. Can't I return the favour?'

'How?! How will you do that? Ten thousand pounds. I need ten thousand pounds to get on my feet again. Have you got it?'

'No, Simon, but...'

'But, what? You'll let me kip at yours? You'll feed me?'

'If I have to. Yes. Yes – I will.'

'You're not being honest.'

He was right. I did not enjoy living with other men – their smells, their habits, the general imposition of it. But how to retract such a friendship-clad assurance? My face matched his statement, so the only way was to be forthright. 'I like the delicateness of women. You know that. But if I have to have a brute roaming the house then preferably it'll be you. I can't say I'll be communicative (I avoided student halls for that very reason). But I hope not to make you uncomfortable.'

'Tell me something…'

'Yes?'

'The drip, drip, drip of your life. How is that better than mine?'

'What do you mean?'

'Going to work. Almost every day. Doing something you're not elated about.'

I didn't need to ask him how he knew that. Sat on the streets he had become a close observer of humans, an anthropologist. It was clear to most people that part of me had died.

'I suppose…' I had to think too much to justify my position. Everything that entered my head sounded forced and trivial. Christ – why did I do it? Did I want beautiful things? Not really. Did I want food, shelter and space? Absolutely. The answer of an ascetic but tinged with frustration and anxiety. Work, mingling with people, scared me to a sufficient degree that becoming directionless *was* a possibility. But the fear, the exposure, the vulnerability of *not* having a cot, a bed, a calm retreat was overwhelming. I could not live like Simon because I was stronger, more resolute, dogged and unbending.

'What I have isn't entirely pretty but I'm at peace in the evenings and at weekends. I feel safe – able to make choices.'

'And that's what you're offering?' He moved his leg perhaps due to numbness. He pushed his spiky, black hair back with the loose fist of his hand.

'It doesn't appear magnificent – I know. But switching the batteries from work to leisure is a blessed and regular relief. To you such a thing is indistinguishable. Just beg, beg, beg.'

I hadn't meant to say the last part. As the words left my mouth they trumpeted a blunt conceitedness. The mood between us immediately darkened.

'You know that? You speak with a certainty encouraged in your world. My pattern, my daily existence...tell me again...beg, beg, beg?!'

'I'm sure it's more...'

'Stay with me for two days and *then* speak...decide what my life's worth. Not before though. Don't be cavalier, impertinent.'

Two days. I couldn't. I would be finished. Lying on the streets in full view of my colleagues – some of whom were bound to pass. No. Not if I claimed to be sick. But days off? Even then...to jeopardise the project. For what? Filth, squalor, indolence. They had my politics neatly sealed and buttoned up.

Expectations went beyond my employer's walls. I was not to embarrass them in any way. Just myself. Here. Now. Purge part of my history. The deterioration in my character was shameful. My personality had been embalmed.

'Simon. I...' I'm a shit head cornered by the burlesque and ballast of my career. I cannot do what I want because the money will dry up. Blood does not flow through our veins but rather currency. 'Is there another way? Can we meet tonight?'

'It's doubtful.'

'Why?'

'I want you to live it...properly. Understand how much of a fraud I feel for taking up space on these streets. Nowhere to go, no aim or mission, apart from footfall and loose change.'

'You've every right. Don't be fooled by respectability...well-dressed people carried away by a sense of their own importance.'

'The stares...'

I gripped his shoulders. Showed him camaraderie. Tried to siphon off that welling up inside him. 'Fuck them! Fuck people who think they're entitled to more. I would reverse the police's role if I could...have them gatecrash swanky, back-slapping functions.'

Where had these words come from? Had I been isolated that much – my indignation tamed? Who was truly begging here, asking for a release from their paltry existence? Myself? Simon? Looking at him, engaging once more with *real* events, I wondered, questioned everything I had built. We're supposed to forget the unfortunate, board the train and head out. So long as we can't *see* their pain, all will be OK. Damn the inquisitive for adding shades of grey.

'I often think back to when I was normal like you are, Gerard. I never gave women a full smile – even then.'

'Why ever not?'

'My plight – I felt it, as early as university. Had no real belief in myself.'

'I think I had optimism then but only because I hadn't met so many people with better memories or a willingness to tolerate drudgery and uninspiring procedural work. Maybe...'

'What?'

'Maybe we let the false world exist because we're not brave enough. The hideous showcasing of politicians, the obligatory applause for business leaders. All of it washing over our TV screens.'

'They don't have televisions out here, so perhaps I'm safe.'

'One of the few advantages, my friend. How do you keep going, keep ploughing on though?'

The question upset him. 'Do you see this as 'going'? Going where?! And ploughing? Certainly not the land. Generalisations, Gerard. I thought you were better than that. Do you not see the anguish?'

It was difficult to speak of such a thing and have people believe you. They thought it theatre of a kind. Anguish? By spelling it out, he risked lessening their sympathy.

Gerard's thoughts hopped around. Of course I see it, came his mind's retort. But why, how, what should I do? I cannot join you – have both of us floundering. What use would that serve? This is a horrible predicament which has me stumbling about.

'I'm offering you a way out. The option of staying at mine. I don't wish to own you or direct you – just merely provide a base.'

'You would really pick me up to that degree?'

Gerard nodded and stared intently at him. They had somehow gone beyond words. Into a flourishing realm. Across a broken and cracked shelf of ice. The air felt warm. Cascades of light seemed to beckon them forth. They both instinctively stood.

'To…not old times, Simon, but a fresh start.'

Simon tried to straighten his clothes. Look the equal of Gerard. It was clear that such an outcome would not occur, yet the effort was worthy of praise.

'I remember, you know. Finishing second.'

'I'm sorry?'

'The Welsh girl – Caitlin. We were both out with her. You charmed her more.'

'More gibberish, I think.'

'It worked though.'

'Yes – for a night. After that, well, she wasn't exactly one I was able to keep.'

It went quiet. Thoughts pervading thoughts. Footsteps even and slow. Gerard hailed him a cab, gave him his keys and made mention of the fridge being full and the water hot. Handing the driver sufficient notes and coins, he let it be known that he would see Simon later.

He thought, as their worlds separated once more, that he desperately needed an arm around himself. Something to check his decline, something to perk him up, make him smile, bring solace to his eyes.

Her Lot (2012)

She knew she had to date bald men and men whose humour was one of ridicule and humiliation. She knew she had to laugh when their eyes wrinkled and they pushed her slightly. She knew that this, somehow, was better than nothing, better than beauty being across from her; its expectations too much to bear.

Once, she had married a busy man, only to have 'angry time' with him in the evenings. After the divorce, she had met a man in Turkey – Samir – while holidaying with her parents. She still had the music cassettes he had given her, the Turkish thrum adding warmth to her flat. She had visited Samir every two months. Had flown out. Shown her independent side. Until. Well, until the incident. She didn't speak of such a thing. Better to bottle it up. Hope the cork holds firm.

She often thought back to when her brain was emptier, easier, less grafted by the optimism of her friends. Now, at times, it was not her in her body but someone else; a hollow remake, a person staring out at the world quite numb.

She didn't expect men she had dreamt of in her twenties. She knew it would be difficult to find someone at her age who wasn't 'wrong', depressed, incompetent, dirty or dull. At 44, she wasn't wholly naïve about that, yet she wondered if someone similar to her existed. Someone nice, once proud, unwilling to cross the (invisible) decent line.

She could be playful, sanguine, sexy even when the mood was right. But it hadn't been right. Not for a while. She supposed that, now, she loved people because they loved her. In her was no dynamic sense of self but a 'go along with it' girl.

She thought of the very average men she was seeing. Yes – two of them. Because even her monogamy was shot through these days. When she was with either one she didn't like lying underneath during sex. It was somehow not dignified, having them slam against her rhythmically. Whilst on top, it meant them clutching at her breasts, but there was an element of control, a 'get out', a vertical prayer of sorts.

After the mature student (who had succeeded the busy man and the Turkish man) she had stumbled upon a fashion catalogue and had learned to dress. Properly. Much sharper. Understand colour. Get laminate flooring in as everyone did at the turn of the millennium. This put her into a new league. One that, unfortunately, her conversation was not ready for.

She supposed that was the time when she knew. To accept her lot. To go back. Try to be at the centre of someone's world. Someone she could trust and laugh at things with.

Now, a decade on and one kidney lighter, she didn't know much anymore. There were the words from one of her better boyfriends: "We're all friggin' insecure. It's only the weasels that aren't." But not much else had stayed with her. Everything, suddenly, had a dark tinge to it. Memories had been creased by her inwardness and introspection. She thought of the shop girl she had once seen staring absentmindedly out of a window. For meaning. For purpose. That was now her, she suspected. Just looking… looking for answers.

There *had* been one – between the fashion of 2002 and the polygamy of 2011. An entreaty from a stranger. A man simply dressed. His telling eyes catching her and then looking away. Not a confident man but one with an inner smile. Neither of them had spoken up though. And then she had alighted. Looked over her shoulder before doing so. Yes – he was watching her depart, following her derrière to the top of the carriage.

She had played it back. Thought his restraint quite charming. Hoped for the same encounter the following day. The day after that even. He never showed up again, however. It was just her fortune to see such a man on his last day of employment. Never to take the same route again. Never to follow her body off the train.

She pleased too many people. That is what boyfriends thought. She had once chatted for thirty minutes upon the telephone ringing in the middle of a DVD. A rather good film had been compromised courtesy of her sympathetic tones to the caller. Mere verbal nodding and supportiveness. A futile conversation when considered properly; one unimportant and disruptive to the evening. When she retook her seat on the couch there was a sense that it would always be like this – her not knowing when to push people away, slide her knickers off and enjoy that before her.

The doctors – her bosses – thought much the same. She was a caring, paediatric nurse, a Florence Nightingale of her day, but time constraints were everything now and so her style, her methods were lambasted. The time spent with parents and relations was frowned upon. She was simply seen as slow, of a past age, not professional enough. Letting down her guard, whilst comforting to Mother and Father who needed someone 'human' in their hour of need, was inefficient, subjective – all those terms which were refractions of goodness.

Often the doctors would shout at her, embarrass her for the tiniest error. A bad fold in the sheets on the bed. Not having the patient's medication to hand even though it was due one hour hence. Doctors could be shits, she thought, with their superior intelligence, their grand lifestyles, the disconnect that swept over them.

"Have you still got hope?" she had once asked a child in earshot of the man in white.

He had grabbed her by the arm and taken her behind a curtain. "What the *fuck* are you asking him that for?"

"We talk frankly with each other. I..."

"Well, not in my hospital! Christ – what is it with you, Yvette..."

She had stayed in the same position for a good few minutes afterwards, weeping. No witnesses. No firmament. Just the muffled response of a woman close to breaking. Dashing to the bathroom to re-do her makeup, she wondered how it had come to this. Unhappiness at home *and* work. Even the silly girls had an outlet, a means of enjoyment. She had takers all around her. It was hard to recall the last time someone had given to her. Whether a compliment, an ounce of understanding or simply just a moment of their time.

In a way, she had entrusted to providence much of her future, but now felt like a fool. Things felt a little flat. She wasn't sure why she did things anymore. What the collection of actions was for. Why get up? Why soldier on? Was she desired? *Really* desired? She suspected she had never been. Just used. Privately mocked. Unable to give out all that was inside her. Something stopped her. From trusting completely. From showing her bare mind.

When she saw other women, comfortable in the presence of handsome men, there wasn't jealousy or envy but rather bemusement. The transient games of the fitter sexes didn't appeal to her. Much better to sign up to a relationship for five years, she thought. But finding that middle man – so difficult. Ironic as well in that she still had her figure. She had heard that some women looked like bowling balls when cutting their toe nails. She continued to sport a lithe, 5'5" graceful frame with an extraordinary set of nipples; assets difficult to conceal and which she was rightfully conscious of.

Away from the titillation though, the chest chicanery, she just wanted to meet someone who was real. It upset her when thinking of her situation. There had been moments in the past when her body simply couldn't cope and so she now kidded her mind. Accepted the brusque arrangements around her. Blanked out the unpalatable.

What had she become? She pushed her lips out so that they sat heavily together and looked down. For a minute – a whole minute – she was at peace. Contemplative. Ruminative. The world…seemed with her. Rearranging her gaze away from the three feet square area before her, however, she soon began to absorb a whirlwind of images.

'No more!' she shouted, in isolation, at home away from the public. 'I have to…'

She knew what she needed to do. First would be the bald man and then the ridicule man. Her lot in life had to be remedied.

He opened the door. She looked at his seemingly mushy and shiny head and then into his eyes. He was plain, not in a kind sense but one which garnered resentment.

'I can't see you anymore.'

'What? We've had fun.'

'I don't think I've ever had fun with you – fun that really involved *me*.'

'So what was the fucking?'

She didn't have an answer. What, indeed, was it? She turned around. He shouted after her: '*What was it*?!'

Ten streets on, she knocked at the remaining house. He came to the door in his dressing gown. It was only 7pm. 'Oh. Did I say tonight?'

He looked a little startled. A female voice followed: 'Who is it?'

'It's over,' she quickly articulated.

'Hey – I say when, honey. I say…'

His sentence faded in her head. She moved away from the miserable crime scene. She would have liked to have said 'Humiliating me – right up until the end' but her own polygamy prevented it.

Done. How did she feel? Still like crying. Not because of them, but...just everything. Who was out there? she thought. Who would save her now? Who could she love?

When she got home she removed her clothes and climbed into bed. Closing her eyes, she tried to imagine something nice. Someone quite magical next to her. Her hands snaked the inside of her thighs. She desperately needed to feel exhilarated. Touching herself, she shuddered slightly. She had largely forgotten how such a thing felt when whispered, done softly.

Samir had asked her to do it. Always insisting that the blanket was pulled back and her eyes firmly shut. He had enjoyed her somewhat reserved moans. Putting her in this situation had made him feel prince-like, powerful, the sexual slayer of white women.

On the seventh occasion, feeling more relaxed and open with him, Yvette had screamed – welcomed in her orgasm. Not hearing the click of a door during her rapture, she had awoken to four bodies stood at the end of the bed.

'Now, for them?' Samir had asked, as if ordering a meal for the younger members of his family.

It still pained her, crucified her, to think of it. As if...as if she was their entertainment. As if privacy meant nothing. Such intimacy given away cheaply. Like an act by a primate in a zoo.

She hadn't known what to do except pull the covers back, prompting giggles and foreign words.

'Get out!' she had shouted. 'Get out!'

They had all left but him.

'Why?' she demanded, physically shaking.

He had just looked at her as if her outburst had shamed him in front of his friends.

'Why?' she asked again, insistently.

'Because I was bored...'

At that he had left. Left her to her tears. Her packing. Her future uncomfortableness with men.

On the plane back, she had asked for a different seat. Away from the random man they had placed her next to. Looking out of the window, she examined the clouds and wondered why, *how* people could be so terrible. Was it as Bertrand Russell had said: "All men are scoundrels, or at any rate almost all. The men who are not must have had unusual luck, both in their birth and in their upbringing."

She still had the letters from the good ones. In a trunk. In the attic. Reading them momentarily cheered her. In her younger self there was something she did not recognise: blind optimism. Now, she was more wary, anxious, concerned as to the information dates might share with her.

So easy to put someone off with a jot of history, a flash of intolerance in the face. The need to run was always high. (Escaping the fitful nightmare that, sat opposite, was usually the wrong person.) On edge, yet hopeful, Yvette pleaded for a crumb of some kind. Not the man who had opened with "They say female donkeys are not as hard working as males." Not the man who had asked her for the exact change to cover the cost of her drink. But someone sweet, caring and funny – yet not in a loud way.

Of late, she had caught herself wishing time away. Thinking ahead to the next good bit of TV or radio. In between there was her own company – something manifestly difficult to bear. And so she often attempted an afternoon nap – setting the alarm clock five minutes ahead of the programme (sufficient time for her to visit the toilet and revive her face with warm water from the tap).

Not entirely 'there' with the programmes, her mind wandered to happenings at work and staccatoed visits to her parents. Picturing herself at the side of a sick child's bed, she could hear her words repeated over and over: "Don't worry. Don't let it worry you." At a point not too long ago – as with *any* job, she convinced herself – the words had become perfunctory. She was no longer saying them in a personal sense, but as a matter of self-survival. Each new case – cancer, leukaemia, hole in the heart – traumatised her and so the distance, the occasional glazed line was necessary.

Easy to tell someone not to worry. Less so with her parents whenever they said she was looking peaky or pallid. "If it means less night shifts, you should change jobs, Yvette." "People don't just switch careers in their forties, Mum." "But the doctors – you've complained about them." "People in power, Mother. People in power."

With that, she had hurriedly left and visited her father. The two of them had divorced fifteen years ago and re-married. Of the respective households, she supposed her father's was more serene and tranquil. In it was the life her mother had stopped him building: shelves full of books; classical music; sufficient space in the kitchen to prevent him from feeling like an intruder; and conversation.

He always greeted Yvette with the same affectionate nuance he had used when she was younger. "Hi, Chicka." This, she didn't so much mind, as grudgingly accept, thinking that in some way it reinforced her precarious and childlike position in the world. Remembering how she used to reach for his hand before asking *the question*, she faltered, waited for him to recollect the same.

"I never got that. You always liked to grab my hand and run. 'Can we run? Can we run, Dad?' Why?"

"Because it was as if I'd become a rocket. Somehow turbo-charged. Faster than everything around me. Invincible."

"Tell me you still feel like that, Yvette, in other ways. Tell me…"

"No. I…I can't. I'm sorry."

In her face was embarrassment, a dawn of sorts, a realisation that she had reached the buffers.

"Hey." He drew her to him and placed his hands on her shoulders. "Don't ever apologise for feeling what we all feel. You need never be unhappy when you're here, you know. We're always a safety net. And if you need me to break through a wall, you know I will."

She was touched. But he was a warehouse man. Not quite…influential. And she had to be realistic. Her family was a modest one. Not one about to change her life. Her lot. Yes – within the confines of this house, this place, she felt proud again, but outside… they would pick her off. People did that. She saw merciless acts almost every day.

"I can't expect you to be with me all the time, Dad. I'm a grown…"

"God damn. What has made you this way? Who has turned…" He petted her. "My girl. You've never shown me this. Whatever it is, Chicka – just get out…"

And so she had. Now she had. Almost remedied the bad things in her life. Shaken off the duplicitous gruff. But the future – what of that?

She couldn't see a new light. She couldn't make out a rare and becoming warmth or incandescence. She knew what people thought of her. And strangely, it might have to be her friends – those who restricted her to timidness – that were given up first. After that, the job, her loose requirements in a boyfriend, so many things that would formerly have dismantled her life.

It would be tough, treacherous. Better to know herself more though. Better to roll to one side on her deathbed and gaze at a loving crowd.

Envy (2012)

If there isn't that empty space between work and home then I am done for, thought Myles Nachman. He did not wish to think about shopping lists or friends or relationships. The odd bust darting in front of him – fine. But heaviness, slammer and demand – no. They should be ushered away.

He walked, after finishing work, down a set of steps, through a revolving door and out along the bustling street. Looking through the numerous shop fronts – too many letting agents to count – he saw bagels, people, stationery, wines, furniture and beds (none of which he wanted). And then he reached the large hotel. The one he resented. The one that steered his frame in all directions - its inconsiderate and incongruous size affecting the weather currents. Especially blowy at the foot of this gargantuan, glass pillar.

Myles slowed down, weighed up the people inside. He could be one of them, in his suit. Except the £8 charge for a beer rather squeezed him out. £4 – that was his absolute top. Anything more was disagreeable, untidy, persecutory.

They always seemed to be discussing essential matters, Myles reflected. And what followed was invariably a laugh, a guffaw, a charged piece of dynamite from each one of them. He wondered if the laugh was aimed at him. It happened so frequently when he passed that he had gotten used to its bite, its caustic tenacity, its damning judgement.

An outsider. A pariah. By his own making. Not just theirs. Even if he *had* money he would not squander it, associate with merry bastards. These fellows – they all looked the same. Grinning gargoyles. Certainty pouring out of them. A shepherd in each pack directing them. If he had a tank, he would drive it through the darkened glass. Uproot them. Make them start again. Established people were somehow the worst. Sure. Patronising. Sealed off from the world. Gandhi had it right travelling third class. You see it then. The full spectrum. The problems. The things that need doing.

Myles didn't understand comfort. Not the ostentatious type. He knew when his body was prostrate, wilting, that he needed space and cleanliness. And when his head was piercing, volcanic, he desired Ibuprofen and silence. But clinical, sterile, gaudy comfort made him question the 'victor' enjoying such wares. They had to be foppish, uncouth, seasoned by Mammon. A little like his brothers.

Why would I want their lives? he often asked himself. Part outrage at the suggestion. Part continued persuasion that he was on the right track. Sure, they have wardrobes I've never seen the likes of – stuffed with jacket after jacket, sweaters that cover eight seasons, not just four – but they've let it get them; the Holidays and Restaurants Brigade.

And more recently, the Private School Crew. A tough alliance. And it's all they ever talk of (foreign countries, food, education). While his own kids were kicking cans around, so the parable went, their cousins were being trained to manage the next generation of irksome saps and oiks.

'*Next door* is for guests,' his younger, Lancashire brother had said, after returning to his farmhouse, pillows out of place, duvet a little ragged. On no account was Myles to sleep in his bed...*ever* again. There were separate quarters – a granny flat – for that. 'Panjandrum,' is how he'd left it. 'You have become a self-important person. I am your brother. We used to share a bunk bed. But I sleep in your bed with my baby son – in the coolest part of the house – and you...you flip. Have a heart attack. Is there nothing of significance in your life? Just the spoils?'

His sister-in-law had intervened at that point. Found his words deeply offensive. And since then Myles had been in hiding. Like a game of silence. Not needing them. Not wanting their stamp on any part of his life. How could it be? Brothers adrift. When... when...they had been so much. His older, London brother too. Courtesy of deleted e-mails. He never read them – Myles's efforts. The job was too big for such trifling piffle. And so, no more. Having your thoughts purged – brotherly tracts (at least from his side) eradicated – was enfeebling, disconcerting. It made him think that no one was listening. Not even his original family. Just expounding their joy and gripes.

They had never understood his life. Why he hadn't come out of the traps at twenty-three, as they had done, and chased the money. Purer, finer ideas – ideology, dare he say – were not credible, realistic. It was just a way of continuing to ostrich his head in the magazines and books, a secret liaison with leisure. When was he going to build, do something tangible? They'd all had shitty jobs – basic accounting, healthcare administrator, data entry clerk, spyhole driller, but young Nachman and old Nachman had solved the grand puzzle, found the code to the safe. Money – easy!

Myles sometimes found himself at the gates of Mammon in his dreams. Bargaining. Negotiating. Trying to come away with his mind intact and his workload reduced. 'If you stop reading the novels and all that political grubbery then we could have a spot for you,' the jewellery-clad, sun-drenched archdeacon would say. 'But that's all I have.' 'Your brothers have done it.' 'No. No. There must have been a different deal. They've always been literary and political atheists.' 'Perhaps you've found the answer then…' 'Yes – to be nothing,' he mumbled to himself. 'Real heroes are dead. Dreaming has become a boy swimming in a cold reservoir.'

He would wake up, not sweating exactly, but disillusioned. These atheists, he thought – would they scream for a god if trapped? Or would the finality of their plight leave them sundered and...reasonable? He had broken off from caring. There were things they *didn't know*. And that was enough. Things they would never have the inclination to find out or enquire about.

Vonnegut, Myles elucidated, *when he was only 21 his mother committed suicide on Mother's Day. Carver – he augmented his craft by working at the Mercy Hospital in Sacramento as a night janitor. After the first hour – jobs out of the way – he would write, let his pen construct new worlds. Sophocles – he wished to be a stage actor but his voice was too weak so he wrote the lines instead. His imagination is said to be one of the finest of all time. Bertrand Russell – only ever* begin *a sentence with 'And'. Don't let it stretch a sentence unnaturally.*

What did they know instead of this? Myles wondered. The carcasses and bones of capitalism? The hissy fits of clients seeking fellatio with every deal? Raw, verbal exchanges behind closed doors? The latest export tariffs?

They knew his ideas – all the family. Brothers. Parents. Cousins. They occasionally got wind of the content of one of his impromptu speeches in the centre of town. A councillor he never became though. Insufficient references to local problems. Instead, moving speeches that belonged to the 1960s. No one wanted them. At times it was like having numerous fire extinguishers sprayed in his face. The dumb stares back and the sodden wit from the crowd infuriated him. Lack of money, however, had been the end result. And that is what counted. The winning post, like much in his life, had eluded him.

'How many is it now, Myles?' his father had asked.

'Three – just three.'

'Three attempts at councillor in about a decade…'

'That would be right.'

'So…time to move on. Try your hand at something else?'

'I haven't thought along those lines.'

'Well, maybe you should.'

Only him. His father had opinions concerning his *un*successful offspring but not the others. 'Shouldn't you be collaring old and young Nachman?'

'I'm not with you, Myles.'

'They're in need of a spiritual base.'

'Always on the soap box, Mylo.'

'Just perturbed.'

'By?'

'My lack of money entitling you to direct my life.'

'Oh, come on – that's hardly fair.'

Perhaps it wasn't, but he had to say it. Let his father understand his black sheep status. That's if he didn't already talk about it with his Saturday night friends. 'Oh, Myles, yeh – still dreaming. Certainly different to the other two. Did we drop him?! No – I don't think so!'

Before the local elections, Myles had gone out on night raids. Posted DVDs in the neighbourhood at 2am. Attempted to politicise the community through Pilger's *War on Democracy*. Gibney's *Enron*, Stone's *Salvador*, and *Americana: The Bill Hicks Story*. There was an article in the *Citizen* after the fifth night, with quotes from the incumbent councillor on his ward: "...we can only assume it's Nachman. This is strong stuff typical of him."

Well, what did they want? *Weak* stuff? Light flicks with the paint brush? The smearing of his sanity followed. He had hoped there were enough in the community to take a chance on him, but clearly there weren't unless there had suddenly been a mass immobilisation. 858 had voted – 48.78% of the eligible people. And his numbers? A miserly 34 (4%).

He put an advert out, asking to meet them. Booked a room above a respectable pub. Wished to brainstorm with his 'party members' about the way forward. Only eleven turned up. He was now down to 1.28% in terms of influence. He looked at them from the mock stage his two friends had built. Weighed up their lives and how similar they were to his. The plan had been to run out on stage, inject a little humour into the proceedings, as if he'd just been given the Democratic nomination in America. At the risk of alienating the few serious individuals who had shown up, however, he'd simply appeared from behind a lifeless curtain and strutted out before them.

'I appreciate you coming. I know that some of you probably have Tory partners. That's the way our wacky society works. It would have bolstered the numbers. And I could have had an argument or two. Still, we're all here and I don't see any evidence of a blue sea, so...'

They were mute. As he was terrible at reading humans and had refused to go on courses to improve such an important characteristic, he gibbered on. It was not polished, particularly self-deprecating, just frank. He had been the oarsman in enough offices to know that bullshit was seethingly despised – a verbal fornicator of audiences. No one appreciated that. Except dumb ass sycophants and climbers.

It was like a jury sat before him with the foreman in the toilet practising his "unanimous" or "majority verdict". "Have you reached your decision?" "We have, Your Honour." "Are you all agreed?" "We are." "Then what say you on the count of speciousness?" "Guilty." "And on the count of falsifying party numbers?" "Guilty."

"34. I *do have* thirty four! How could I rig the ballots?"

"*Quiet!!* Myles Nachman – you have been found guilty on two counts. Both of them carry a heavy sentence, a means of repaying the community you have abused. From here you will be taken to a maximum security prison, housed in a call centre, made to work 10 hours a day for a period of…"

He blinked. A long, heavy blink. He was not envious of his brothers. He could not be. Just look at the wives. Such pulchritude in his. And theirs? Fussing ad nauseam. Incessant shopping. Chicken-wing breasts. The personality of a jug of Vimto. Glee bought from Waitrose. He could not lie next to them, be isolated with either at *any time* of the day. Nor could he show his deeper thoughts around them.

Old Nachman took statins, not because of his younger wife, but because he had made it to partner in an LLP and wished to continue extracting the booty without an interim clutching of the heart. His house was the size of Gene Wilder's chocolate factory, but was strangely missing a centre. Myles had visited only once and had asked to be shown Speakers' Corner in Hyde Park only to be driven to a pizza joint. He let it go, just as he let their general reticence pass without getting too heated. Words were not theirs as they were his. Hollywood films sufficed and other such cultural paucity.

And yet – they were free men. They could both get out now were it not for their clawing wives. Myles regularly estimated their respective wealth based on discreet chats with Mother Nachman, together with subtle questions about retirement. Old Nachman had to be worth £3m including the London property. Young Nachman – perhaps he was touching £1m.

It hit Myles that he would live by others' rules longer than them. He would cart around, lift, bow, grimace at filthy individuals above him. Need their approval, their sign off for the slightest decision. While his brothers – they had the zeros required. They could laugh heartily in Italian restaurants. Throw £20 notes around. Put petrol in their cars as if it was gravy.

Damn – am I breaking? thought Myles. Am I reaching the point I never thought I'd reach? He stumbled. All of a sudden thought his politics useless, threatening for not making him comfortable. No wonder the *hard left* were smokers and drinkers – unlike him – because dying young was one way to escape the torture; perhaps the first rule in their secret constitution.

The terrible road or juncture – he had reached it, gasped at his brothers' accumulation of money, the phenomenal interest earned; their consequent domination, playboy lifestyles, only with family in tow. Often Myles thought (elbows hard against his work desk): These appear to be dead people I'm working with. Their gaze is off centre. Their conversation is propped up by sardonic nothingness. Their habits are those of pickled commoners. Perhaps I ought to have got a career, he mused. Or taken more chances in my twenties. His life, as it stood, was a permanent horror film – full of suspect make-up, histrionics and average Joes actually *believing* they were close to the pinnacle of existence. You *fuckers!* he felt like shouting almost daily. You rabid, banal halfwits. Knowing is not *knowing*. It is a small dance; a mere meeting of hands.

What have I actually picked up over the years though? wondered Myles. So many magazines, broadsheets and Berliner-size newspapers, yet I am stuck. He looked at his hands. They were relatively small, unblemished. He hadn't used them enough – shown his complete repertoire. I have depended on my father too much, not sought his skills, thinking….thinking what? That I am too good to get dirty? Steinbeck would have slapped me in the face. Had me build a tree house before my next meal.

He thought of all the jobs he had watched being done: repairing a puncture; papering and decorating; bricklaying; messing with the car; plumbing; concreting the driveway; simple electronics / soldering. He was ashamed. He could quote lines from Martin Luther King Jr speeches, but on a practical level he was a chump.

He would get the train down, he decided. To his brother's in London for the second time. The invite had been sitting there for months and so now – while at his lowest – he would venture out, try to see something. Not the sights, but a different world. Try to understand how old Nachman did it – added the zeros, remained calm in this shitty world. He knew his brother could be phlegmatic, controlled, but there had to be more to it. A brain – yes. One that turned as regularly as Jupiter. Not like his own with the slower rotation span of Mercury.

He would watch him while they ate. Ascertain how he chewed. Whether there were special creases in his pants. Galton's research had shown that half of all first borns were furtively given the brains and had been part of an unequal cake cutting ceremony before the race had even begun. Perhaps he would mention this. Perhaps he would make a claim on certain assets. No – entitlement would cheapen his visit, leave him locked in a Zarkanaian stew. He had to go in unruffled with a certain repose. Shake hands like they were...well, they *were* brothers. Often it took a bit of remembering given the drift in recent years. If he was to break down, perhaps fall at the feet of the millionaire – beg for a quarter million – then it would have to be in the evening. After a few drinks. Once base had been touched. Once old Nachman saw the struggle in his eyes, the pitiful state of the next in line, the blundering expression disguising everything apart from his predicament.

The station pick up had been clean. Myles felt the plushness of his brother's life as soon as he opened the black car door. No squeaks. No running for the WD-40. No litter strewn at the foot of the passenger. Just impeccability, with a refined voice welcoming him.

'You made it.'

'Yes.'

'Hungry?'

'Ravished.'

That happened. He had meant to say 'ravenous', but his words had gotten mixed up. They often did in the company of people he rarely saw.

Old Nachman appeared not to notice. 'Good – Sophie's got one of her risottos on.'

It was hilly, where they lived. Near a large green. The ragwort was out in huge numbers, as it was back home (somehow more than a weed). The people here seemed to have a different stride, a confidence, a laissez faire grandiosity. Myles noticed the coffee houses, the flower shops, the salons, the Victorian pubs, the sweet, infested bookshops. He passed by people whose raison d'être appeared to be LIVE NOW, CHALLENGE

NOTHING, WORK WITHIN. Their laces were tighter, their shoulders more athletic, their smiles pleasantly fixed. Each and every driveway on this final leg was carefully and expensively patterned and bricked. 'Tarmac' was a word uttered in other neighbourhoods. Not this. Not among the fine people of Chimpledon.

His brother pulled in. Tinkered around with the position of the car. Surprisingly opted *not* to use the double driveway, but instead park on the road. They got out. Old Nachman grabbed one of the bags without being asked – led Myles to the gothic front door. There was no swagger, no "look at what I got", just homewardness. He was still a Nachman. Myles could see that. Modesty pouring out of him. But once inside, he saw how the art had eaten him up – precious and pointless Bateman cartoons from the 1930s lining the walls, modernity courtesy of provocative female rears.

Myles was dreading his face to face with Sophie. The last time they'd met had been at young Nachman's where she had greeted his arrival with a fretful countenance. Somehow, in her eyes, he was a purveyor of controversy, an excited little boy not in the real world.

His brother introduced him: 'Here he is.'

Myles wandered into the anticipated fray expecting daggers and cold heartedness.

Somewhat unusually, she was accommodating, quick to fling her arms around him.

'Brother-in-law,' she whimsically corralled him with. 'You must be tired. Sit down. Sit down. A drink?'

He asked for a beer, the cleanness of Peroni, which was immediately thrust into his palm. Sipping it, he looked around, rejoiced in the freedom of being a guest. His nephew would be here soon, ready to bombard him with overt questions. He liked him, if at the same time grievous with concern over his upbringing; the Fruit Winder breakfasts, excessive exposure to Disney films, and tiny attunement to the concept of money.

Perhaps in old Nachman's position Myles would be a similar parent. When something is easy to come by, easy to fish out of the world, you don't think of it that much. Hence, his nephew's agreeable but skewed relationship with money. This and the forcefulness of a leisure-indulgent wife had probably led to his brother's cultural looseness, his difficulty in exerting solid boundaries.

'Charlie won't be joining us, Myles. He's staying at his friend's.'

'Oh, right. Tomorrow though?'

'Yes. Certainly.'

'Just us then?'

'I hope that's OK…'

It wouldn't be as playful without Charlie around, as chatty. The air might even be thinner. But Myles would have to make do, hope the spectre of previous hostilities did not return.

'I meant to say, before we get started…these letters you've been sending him…I'm not sure they're what he needs.'

'Needs?'

'Yes. What you're telling him about…'

'Guy Fawkes?'

'Yes. That's him. They don't follow the formal route.'

Myles nodded. He'd like to at least start the meal and a second beer before laying into her. He'd like to point out what made him warm under their roof.

Dinner was to be served. They clinked their wine glasses from behind the work unit before joining him. It was a gesture old Nachman looked uncomfortable with but he did it because he was now in a different world, a higher league. The little things. You had to be *with* the etiquette, hinged to its evolution. You had to observe what the other couples did for kicks.

Myles smiled wryly inside. He could never indulge in such a congratulatory gesture. Except at weddings, anniversaries and birthdays. His enmity towards the wealthy somehow spiked upon witnessing such things.

'He was a Catholic, Sophie – a persecuted Catholic.'

'Who?'

'Fawkes.'

She lifted her nose to indicate an understanding, an acknowledgement that was to go no further. Through her contact lenses came a subtle rebuke. Old Nachman's shifting religious affiliation, the scraping of his knees for this woman, made such an outcome difficult, however.

His brother patted his back, offered a clipped yet jocular resolution: 'We'd rather our son wasn't radicalised just yet, Myles...'

The al dente of the rice momentarily seduced Nachman. He smiled. Didn't wish to upset anyone. Loathed the possibility of feelings being crumpled. If he was honest, he would admit that old Nachman had given their lineage property and guile, a much needed polish, whereas he had perhaps only taken the name down, close to begging, occasionally accepting second-hand clothes.

He could buy this, wander into the store they were touting, if it wasn't for the...hiatus in old Nachman's learning. Impressive 'O' and 'A' levels in history had dotted – nay, chiselled – his brother's past, but now...now? It was evident that he didn't care for such 'grotesque' reasoning. Curiosity had been wiped from his, *their* mindsets. They had become part of a *captured class*, bought off and shorn of any depth. Comfort. In their eyes it had surpassed muck-raking, done away with the pernicious selfishness of public opinion.

The evening closed in. Sophie left them to their cigars and spite. Myles had to speak, address his brother as if they were twenty again. Frankness. Tough talk. Nothing to lose – except elevated egos.

'I wish you would reply to my e-mails. I'm lucky if I get one in ten back.'

'You know the reason for that. Always controversial. Do you have *any other* gear?'

The drink. It was loosening them. Making them sloppy and tactless. Varnishing over their deeds and actions.

'I just like to ask questions. Bloody questions, that's all.'

'Yes – about where I stand on tax evasion.'

'You make it sound so polite.'

'Myles. Myles. We're not playing now. Such a remark could have got me sacked. Jeopardised my family's future.'

'Two types of people, David – the avaricious and the altruistic. The first group think it dignified to be concerned about *their taxes* only. Which are you?'

'You're in *my* house, Myles. Time to stop this...'

'Censorship! Rules! When did you let it draw you in, David? Were you even conscious of it?'

'No. No. Not in here.'

'Outside then...'

Old Nachman stood in front of him. Spoke only inches from his face. 'I thought you came down here for direction. The man I spoke to was...'

'A little bloodied by life?'

'If that's how you want to put it, then yes.'

'So how were you gonna fix me, David? Did the risotto have something in it?'

He weighed him up. Looked at his younger brother. Thought how despondent he had become. Idealism can kill a man, he thought. Paw at his insides. Despatch what sensibilities he might have had.

'We're all...dissatisfied, Myles. It didn't quite become what we imagined. But...you fight.'

'I've done that. It hasn't worked. I've followed what I thought I was meant to do. Failure though. *Fucking* failure.'

'I don't know what to say.'

Why did I come down? thought Myles – expose myself to this phlegmatic ordeal. Wandering around the house he realised he wasn't part of their life. There were no photos of him, no obvious mementos. Not even a snap of old Nachman's nephews; Charlie's cousins.

Back home Myles had a treasured photo of himself and his two brothers. They must have been 15, 18 and 21 – stood on the patio beaming and sulking. Youth...about to go through the door, stake its claim, find a pleasant corner of the world. Here, he had been deleted, purged, like the e-mails. They didn't need his face because it held them back, gave less warmth than their son.

Myles stared at David. He only knew a little bit of him now. Foolish to expect more, he thought. Foolish.

Did he envy him? Just a long, choked up silence inside.

Homage to Hernandez (2017)

'Who's James Dean?'

She surprised you like that – seemingly did not know any of the cultural icons of the last half century. And yet her sparkle, her vibrancy, the keenness of her eyes and smile made you want to be around her.

She was a truck in motion – a misunderstood, elegant force, a surging dynamo ready to shunt you off the road or consume you eagerly.

When she fell, fell for something she didn't expect, she gave that object of desire all of her being: nakedness; fire; laughter; and words - words that rolled out in unaccustomed patterns.

Before now, before the meeting in the porch, before she had chosen her affair, she had been existing - just existing. A loyal, family spouse doing what others required of her. But slowly dying inside.

She joked about her new man – called him a toff, gave him the name Darcy in an effort to immortalise the stiff, yet endearing fibres within him.

How had this come about? Why had two steady, married individuals decided to unfurl their lives in a half-abandoned, reckless fashion which, to some, spoke of madness?

Because each of them were thirsty. Each of them needed a unique, intimate adventure that awakened a neglected part of them. Each of them needed to *feel* a deep, blissful harmony.

It was probably supposed to be a fling – a few exciting encounters that rejuvenated them, gave them respite from their respective marriages. But what they found was a soaring compatibility, something that hurt when they were apart because when they gazed at each other they knew that they had stumbled upon an ineffable love, a timeless thrill which separated them from the world – cast them adrift on a dreamy, edgeless island.

'He's Mr White T-Shirt. I thought you liked white T-shirts?'

'I do, but...'

For once, she was caught cold. The gregarious girl with tousled, dark red hair and a delicious attitude had fallen over her own supposed passion. It was like Arthur Miller thinking that Marilyn Monroe had sung for Abraham Lincoln the year after their divorce.

'Absurd! It's absurd. Where have you been for the last three decades, Hernandez?'

Hernandez. That name. The name he had given her due to her Spanish roots and the coded communication it afforded them. D & H. H & D. He would let her initial go first because she was a bossy

5' 2" munchkin of a woman, an Oompa Loompa he claimed, rejected by Gene Wilder and the cast of *Charlie and the Chocolate Factory* simply because she was too beautiful.

She liked this. Her exterior suggested that even a minimal comparison was wounding, but underneath she respected a man that was able, through playful, inverted warmth, to put her down or at least challenge the image she had of herself.

'In a bubble. I've always been in a bubble. Where it's safe. My parents will tell you that. How I got eight GCSEs, I don't know.'

The laugh that followed Hernandez's sentences was infectious. It was giddy, inviting, a flare of sorts. You could not miss or ignore this woman. She was there to be analysed, worshipped and stripped. Something in her had remained when all other adults were disrobing their character and lazily entering the manufactured landscape.

Darcy was more than alive when he was with this woman. He was fitful, distracted, yet oddly calm and whole. He often thought to himself: Was it *really* possible to meet a woman in another man's porch?

Because that is how this had come about. Ridiculously so. Curiously looking up at her petite frame given the 12-inch step. And now she was at least *infrequently* throwing words at him, exploring herself, telling him how it felt to be part of what they had: Spontaneous, exciting, adrenaline-like, romantic, fun, loving, orgasmic, tender, dreamy, rude.

Hernandez did that. She saved the word that would flatten him, metaphorically cup his balls 'til last. Rude. It *was* rude, but delightfully so. They were physically joined every time they met. They were snog-meisters if such a thing was permitted at their age (39 and 45 respectively).

They would bound down hotel corridors, occasionally take the lift against the advice of her heart specialist. But only so she could reflect how it felt afterwards having finally retreated from the dangerous public gaze with her illicit man. 'My heart was beating like the clappers in the lift when you kissed me.'

Clichés turned into sensual riffs when passing Hernandez's lips. They − or rather the word "clappers" − somehow took on a symphonic quality, a heightened grace that deplored inertia.

The word 'GO' was at the core of Hernandez. She was always planning, loving, enjoying what she could, however demanding that activity was against the backdrop of her tapered-down marriage.

This bewildered Darcy. He had always gone for quiet girls − perhaps more malleable creations. Hernandez's fire, her cute, Weeble-like movement, made him reassess or rather dismiss a 'type' he may have had in his head.

Love kills you. It knocks you over. It arrives and you can do nothing about it. You cannot quantify it. You cannot comb over its finer points except to say that in its company you are mesmerised and comfortable.

When Hernandez looked at Darcy – for however many seconds he was fortunate to hold that stare – the centre of the universe was his. He had met something, some*one* so uplifting and rousing that the prospect of ever losing her was too much for his simple, ragged heart.

The crazy thing was, he *liked* nakedness from her, but he sensed he did not need it. The nakedness of her face was enough – wrapped as it was just above the neck line of her many splendid coats. Something about this woman was so radiant and becoming that winter added a glow to her.

In the shimmering light of her green and brown-tinged eyes and red lips was some kind of daft and sexy undiscovered life. While the scientists were busy scouring the moon and Mars for rock particles, they had neglected to notice Darcy's girl, his wondrous, part-time puss, his morning, noon and night.

He remembered some of the lines she had written and spoke - not *showed* him as she preferred, but actually laid before him and wired up (braved what she believed was her autistic streak carved from her trying past and DNA): 'Pobrecito novio...You make me smile and drive me wild...I totally lose myself with you...Your laugh warms me like hot, sticky toffee pudding...Crazy how it's developed so quickly.'

They were not Darcy words. He was a literary man, a '"pompous twit" as she liked to remind him, but how could he not fall into her when she stood before him so magnificently and manifestly unarmed and alluring.

Whatever it was that she had mined in him, got her archaeological charm to dig out, would have certainly stayed there – never to be discovered – if it weren't for her prettiness and rapture.

When I do ordinary things, I think of her, Darcy realised. I think of her because she offsets this wooden life. She compensates for the hurt I see around me – the hurt *inside* me. I wish to be with her more than I can.

Am I guilty of being effusive? he asked himself. Of perhaps embellishing or decorating what we have? No! he insisted. In the moments when we are hot, when we grapple for each other like alley cats, I feel *together* yet out of myself, expressive like never before.

She has opened part of me up, removed my stiffness with her straight-talking, her sexual clamour, her beautiful, demanding rumpus and hullabaloo. When she is in my lap completely abandoned, I wish to freeze time, suck on her nips, hold her against me, feel our fit, our jigsawed bodies, as if...as if there will be no one else again.

I want that. I really do. To discard every other adult when I am with this woman. To play with her ears, her neck, watch her eyes when they develop that dark, lustful need, that filthy, demanding stare which orders me to satisfy her.

Look. Look what we have done. How we have acted. We have been furtive, secretive, but also bold, risk-laden lunatics. In desperate pursuit of each other – sat in our cars next to industrial bins (that first night when I opened her door and was met by that maiden smile).

Other, prettier stuff as well, finer locations: picnics against the backdrop of wild, dense country; tiny, neglected lanes after work where two cars are but the prescient and rudimentary transporters of naked frames that need to latch on to each other for sustenance and fortitude; bike rides adjacent to the Irish sea where seagulls despair but Darcy and Hernandez talk about nothing and everything.

I have even followed her into shops and exercise classes where we have both been aware of each other's presence and it has been intoxicating, fulminating, like a feast laid before ravenous wolves.

'You're going to get it Thursday.' Just one of her many rejoinders, a throwaway line which spoke of how they were going to use their brief, stolen time together.

What other woman could tell him what he was going to *get*, what he was going to be sexually enslaved *to*? Only Hernandez. And if he asked of her only glasses on her person and nakedness, she would willingly acquiesce.

Darcy pictured this woman constantly. She dominated his mind, his thoughts, the neurological charge within him. She was wild, but refreshing. There was nothing staged or contrived about her. The pictures she sent him – in between their rendezvous – were not from a favoured angle of her face, but rather a giving, compromised, *every woman* slant; one which brandished her wares, her features in the manner of an organic, jungle creature.

Sassy was the one, single word that encapsulated and explained Hernandez, Darcy decided. She *was* that. All of that. *Confident. Spirited.* And *cheeky*. And yet, within her, beyond that toughness, that "Rottweiler" exterior she unfairly and protectively labelled, was a child; a child that had perhaps given too much comfort to others and now guiltily sought comfort and adventure herself.

What other woman in her cute blundering when Darcy amusingly enquired as to whether there would be a fanfare to greet him the next time they met could confuse a loud blast of brass instruments with a can of Fanta!

'*Fanta*?! No. No. Fan*fare*! I have no need to drink carbonated orange when I'm with you, Hernandez.'

Who else made him laugh like that? Who else plucked at his heart strings with great, genuine gaffs and a look that locked his eyes? In her dizziness, her brashness, her soft, soft moments, her kaleidoscopic patterns, Hernandez blew him away. She completely had his defences down.

'I bet you go off me when you see me with hat hair.'

Darcy, being the slight toff that he was, had never heard such an expression. But when he looked carefully at her across the restaurant table and took in the flat fringe and sequestered curls, he realised what she was referring to.

She *did* look different. She looked plain and *without* those rich, tousled locks. But in that plainness was something he had only on a few occasions noticed before (ahead of her beauty). In that plainness was honesty and virtue and warmth, and he shook himself for not fully recognising such solidity and rectitude.

But their lives away from the fun and tingle: one child each. Her, an eleven-year-old son. Him, a thirteen-year-old daughter. Did that impact their plans, their far-reaching dreams which stood like dots on the horizon?

There are periods, thought Darcy – periods when we seem to know, when sadness envelops us because we know at best we can only be together in five years. And what can five years do to a part-time affair? What can it implement and bend and torture?

We both know we are struggling now. Despite the mutual fascination. Despite the harmony which cossets us like a giant blanket. We both have partners – a wife and a husband. And families that need stability – children that need Mum and Dad and not intruders. That is what good people do – they do not break such things.

But at some point don't you live for yourself, what you recognise as your inherent need, because those around you will feel that joy rather than the dutiful mediocrity that old marriages bring, rather than the dejected face of a child that sees his parents as a miserable, coupled-up template?

Darcy probably pushed for this more. Not because he loved his daughter less, but because the ache inside him was too pure and knowing and gripped by the futile road ahead of him.

Hernandez hadn't just given him his name, she had *created* Darcy, pulled him from a skip, abolished everything in him that no longer believed in relationships, man and woman, Adam and Eve.

She played this down, claimed that he saw something in her that did not exist, that was not particularly exceptional. But it is up to a man's eyes, ears and lips to interpret that before him. And Hernandez...well...she was like no other.

'My passion and love are with you,' she told Darcy when discussing very loosely what went on behind their respective closed doors, how horrible seeds and thoughts sometimes penetrated the brain.

'I orgasm just at you brushing past me, I want you that bad,' she further extolled.

But such barricades could not keep out the inevitable day. The day when emotions snowballed and the double life became too much.

It was Hernandez who phoned twelve days before Christmas (on the damn 13th). Hernandez who broke down because she was "torn", wavering, irresolute, vacillating – all those words that did not belong to her and had no place in her normally steely deportment.

A combination of tachycardia, insomnia, knots in her stomach, worries over her son and family finding out, and Xmas morality had weighed her down, "eaten" her up, meant that juggling Darcy had become too much. He was good for her health, but also bad it seemed. Bad while she had a young child and was married. Bad because him being a handsome distraction filled her life with too much.

'If circumstances were different…'

Circumstances. That word kept cropping up in their final few texts and conversations. And for the first time Darcy flipped.

Circumstances! What right does such a feeble word have to de-rail Hernandez and I?!!!! Fack circumstances! Kick it outside! Circumstances should never be able to ride roughshod over something so carefully and wonderfully built.

In the days after, ticking clocks seemed to harden the silence. Darcy cried at random times now. He was, in a sense, no more. Empty. Just empty now. Empty of the chivalry she had pulled from him.

He could not even get his staple diet of words out. Instead it was just aches, verbal monstrosities and indescribable moans.

'I can tell you anything,' she had cried down the phone in a stuttered fashion on the night she had rubbed out the letter 'H' from 'H & D', the night she had un-engraved their togetherness from the world's canvas.

If that is so, thought Darcy, then why are we here in this deep, deep hole?! *Why!!!* he nearly screamed at the clouds.

'Don't change who you are.' Another well-meaning but apocalyptic sentence from Hernandez.

How could he *not* change? He would eventually go mad without this woman. Find himself in a padded cell.

We're all asked to do certain things in life: be loyal; honourable; and civilised. Darcy, despite the good, early reports on his character now decided that he could no longer be civil. He would rather withdraw from the world without Hernandez. He would rather make friends with his pillow. Because images were all he had now. Images in his head of her beauty, her slender arms, her sublime, tousled hair and eyes.

If there was one hope left it was that she could no longer accept her old self. That while she was sat in the company of her wider family and friends during the festive period, she wished and wanted him in the chair next to her; so much so that maybe holding her again *was* possible.

If that was not to be, thought Darcy, then the "Glow Cops" (those imaginary detectives they had invented who notice a sudden surge of unexplained happiness in people) can just retire. Because there will never be a glow again. There will never be spontaneity, excitement, adrenaline, romance, fun, love, orgasmic joy, tenderness, dreaminess and rudeness.

Only a gaping hole. A space that she, for fifteen weeks, filled so exquisitely.

Printed in Great Britain
by Amazon